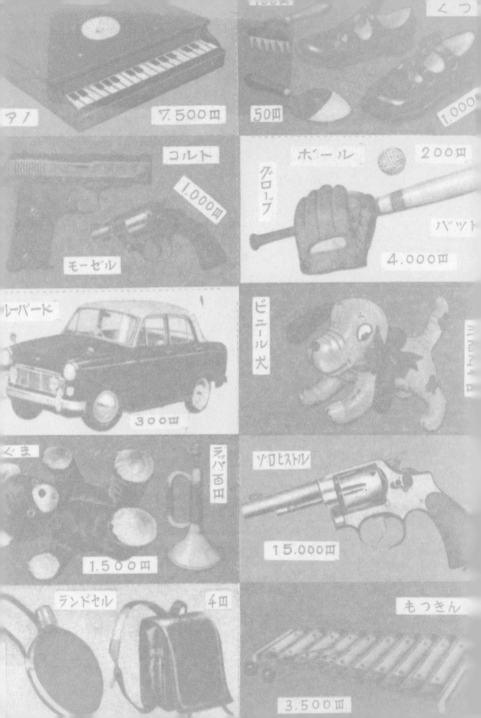

アノ　7.500円

くつ　50円　1.000

コルト　1.000円
モーゼル

ボール　200円
グローブ
バット　4.000円

レーバード　300円

ビニール犬

ぐま　ラッパ百円　1.500円

ゾロヒストル　15.000円

ランドセル　4円

もつきん　3.500円

Twinkle Twinkle

KAORI EKUNI

TRANSLATED BY EMI SHIMOKAWA

VERTICAL.

Published by Vertical, Inc., New York.

Originally published in Japan as *Kira Kira Hikaru* by Shinchosha, Tokyo, 1991.

ISBN 1-932234-01-2

Manufactured in the United States of America

Book design by Studio 5E

First American Edition

Vertical, Inc.
257 Park Avenue South, 8th Floor
New York, NY 10010
www.vertical-inc.com

TABLE OF CONTENTS

EMBRACING WATER

• •

Every night, Mutsuki stepped out to gaze at the stars before he went to bed. He was convinced the habit was responsible for his good eyesight, 15/20 in each eye. I went out onto the veranda too—not to look at the stars, but to look at Mutsuki. I loved watching his face as he gazed at the starlit sky. He had a beautiful face, with short straight eyelashes.

"What're you thinking about?" he asked.

"Life," I said. I'd meant it as a joke, but Mutsuki nodded seriously. These were my happiest moments—out on the veranda with my husband, a glass of Irish whiskey in my hand, the night air cool against my skin.

But I could never stay out long before I felt the cold.

I hurried back into the warm apartment and came face-to-face with the purple man. He was a watercolor. Most of his aging face was buried in a big bushy beard. I stood in front of the painting and sang. You see, the purple man liked to hear me sing.

After treating him to two verses of "It's Raining Tonight, Mr. Moon," I went into the bedroom and plugged in the mottled black and white cord and waited. After a while, I folded back the covers and ran the hot iron over the sheets from one corner of the bed to the other. I didn't hum as I did when I smoothed out wrinkles from my laundry. I focused on what I was doing. This was serious work; speed was key. It was the one household chore Mutsuki demanded of me.

I briskly pulled backed the covers and unplugged the iron.

"Ready!"

Our marriage was ten days old—but explaining our marriage is no simple matter.

"Thanks," Mutsuki said with his usual smile and got in between the warm sheets.

I do translation work from Italian, as a kind of part-time job. Since it was about time I finished up with an interview piece I'd been nibbling at all week, I turned off the bedroom lights, closed the door, and went and sat down at my desk.

I poured myself some whiskey, freely. That deep, rich hue of gold—what a way it had of entrancing me.

"Alcoholism? I don't think you need to worry about that!" the doctor had dismissed, laughing. "Your liver is fine, and your stomach too. You're having only two or three drinks a day, after all." When I told him I couldn't quit, he got up and patted me on the back. "I'm sure it's a passing fancy. And remember, Jesus thought it all right to take a little wine for your health," he said. "I'm giving you some vitamins. Just try not to worry yourself sick."

"Try not to worry yourself sick," I imitated the doctor out loud, swilling my glass.

All of a sudden, I felt that I was being watched. I turned around to look: it was the *yucca elephantipes* staring over at me. The "Tree of Youth"—the potted plant's bizarre alias—was a wedding gift from Kon. With its dense foliage of large, sharp, straight leaves, it seemed eager to pick a fight.

I glared back at Kon's tree and downed the rest of my whiskey.

Mutsuki was already in the kitchen when I woke up.

"Morning. You want me to fry you up some eggs?"

I shook my head.

"An orange maybe?"

"Yes please."

By the time I was back from my morning shower, Mutsuki had done the dishes. On a glass plate he had set out for me was an orange, sliced into comb shapes, dripping with juice.

As I sat eating, Mutsuki programmed the heater to keep the room temperature stable and picked out the day's background music for me.

I filled a cup and watered the Tree of Youth. Through the

blinds the morning sun drew bright stripes on the carpet. The water sounded delicious as it hissed through the soil.

"Tell me about Kon," I pestered.

"When I get home," replied Mutsuki.

Mutsuki, who was a doctor, drove off every morning at 9:10 on the dot. Apart from night shifts, his weekly cycle was a regular salaried man's, with a two-day weekend.

Having seen off my husband, and having skimmed the papers, I decided to finish up the interview, which I hadn't done the night before. I was still feeling unwell from having translated the fashion designer (with a Milanese address) confess to an "inability to love anything that is not beautiful," when the phone rang. My mother called me almost every day.

"Feeling fine?"

She sounded so concerned that I became a little irritated and snapped at her. "Fine? What do you mean, 'fine'?"

At the top of the bedroom chest, along with the VCR instruction manual, my marriage ring warranty and the lease for our apartment, were two medical reports. My mother's voice tended to remind me of them. True, she knew only about one: the self-contradictory certificate according to which my *mental illness was nothing abnormal*. "The term 'mental illness' covers such a wide range of conditions, you see," the dunce of a doctor had explained. "You aren't *not* suffering from mental illness. Don't worry, though—it's no more than a case of emotional instability. Your drinking is probably a manifestation of it. I'm sure you'd start feeling better in no time if—and I say this just for instance—you got married." If you got married! His irresponsible advice was to blame for seven meetings with potential marriage partners.

"What's wrong? Sounds like you're in a bad mood," my mother said.

"Not really. It's just that I was in the middle of work." I carried the phone into the kitchen and took a can of peach fizz from the fridge. I opened the can with my free hand.

"That's good, but make sure you get housework done, too," my mother said. "Don't drink too much. Your father and I will come see you soon. Say hi to Mutsuki from me." I hung up the phone. I threw the can into the trash bin.

My mother was overjoyed when she learned that Mutsuki was a doctor. And not because of status or salary. Scrutinizing a photo of Mutsuki, she had said, quite in earnest: "You're going to get better, my dear, living with a doctor."

When I told Mutsuki about that, on one of our first dates, he laughed heartily. "So I guess we've both got something to hide," he had said. "Ha, ha, ha, a couple of partners in crime."

That's why I dread my mother's phone calls. They make me mull over things I'd rather forget. The thing is, you see, Mutsuki doesn't like sleeping with women. In fact, he doesn't so much as kiss me. So you see how things stand. Yes, alcoholic wife and gay husband—real partners in crime!

"So, what would you like to hear about?" Mutsuki said. "The movies I saw with Kon? The time he and I went to the beach?"

It was cold out on the veranda, and the blanket I had wrapped around my shoulders dragged like the Little Prince's mantle. I sipped my whiskey.

"Tell me about when you went to the mountains."

"Can't—we never did," Mutsuki laughed.

"Then tell me how Kon fought it out with a cat."

"But I just told you that one."

"Encore, encore," I said, giving my glass a shake and rattling the ice by way of applause. Mutsuki took a long draught from his bottle of Evian and began his tale.

"Kon had this Shiba dog called 'Koro' ever since it was a puppy. He had a rule in dealing with it: whenever he had to scold Koro, or just got mad at it for some reason, he always had to get down on all fours first. He didn't think it was fair to yell down at the dog from on high, up on two feet, or to hit it with his free 'front paws,' meaning his hands. Kon was quite serious about these match-ups. From Koro's point of view, though, Kon was an old buddy, so the dueling never escalated beyond rolling around on the floor. But one day, when Kon came over to my place—and I had a cat back then, I guess about five years ago, when I lived in Ogikubo—somehow or other Kon had gotten down on all fours and was suddenly lunging at my cat. Obviously, I'm pretty surprised by what's happening. But not as surprised as my cat. Her name was Garbo. And Garbo, who's excited, has no qualms about using her hands. And unlike dogs, of course, she's pretty good with them. Better than people, even. And what's more, she has claws. By the end Kon's face is covered in blood like some villain's at the end of a samurai drama. It was pretty bad, really."

He took a big gulp of his Evian and closed his eyes nostalgically. I was very happy with Mutsuki, who retold a story without skimping on the details.

Two days after the deadline, I finally handed the manuscript to my editor at a coffee shop by the train station. It was such a wonderful clear day that I turned my walk home into a little promenade, only to find Mutsuki's father waiting by our door when I finally came home. Seeing me, he raised a hand and grinned.

"Good timing! I was just thinking to go if nobody was home." His beaming smile belied the depressing connotation of the term "middle-aged."

I told him I was sorry, I was out for a walk, Mutsuki was still at work—while I unlocked the door, laid out a pair of slippers, and poured some whole-grain tea.

"Oh I'm fine, don't bother. Just dropped by to see how

things were going."

I tensed up. Like what things? Mutsuki's mother and my parents had agreed to our marriage as a great idea; only my future father-in-law had objected, and here he was.

"You know what, I think I like this room," he said.

"Yes, I'm very grateful." As soon as the words escaped my mouth, I thought "Wow, there's servility for you."

"So you've gone ahead with it," my father-in-law suddenly cut to the point. "You know, it's when I think of your parents that I feel terrible."

"Oh, you shouldn't feel that way, really. They're very happy."

"Because they don't know."

Here it comes, I thought, the question of the other medical report: *Our tests indicate that you are HIV negative.*

Luckily I caught myself in time before blurting out, "True, my parents didn't know, but we too, for our part...." I couldn't very well tell him the score was, actually, even. My "emotional instability" was a secret.

"Marry *him*? Must be like embracing water."

When he said this, I felt a cool, rustling presence at my back. I didn't have to turn around to figure out what it was. I spoke loud and clear so the tree could hear too: "It's okay. I never really liked sex that much anyway."

My father-in-law seemed taken aback for a second, but soon let out a little laugh.

I seized the chance to clear the air. In a fluster I stood up and asked, "Shall I put on some music?"

I grabbed a CD at random from Mutsuki's collection and placed it on the player.

"Your tea's cooled off," I declared, "let me pour you a fresh hot cup."

Explosions of sound filled the air.

"You like opera?" my father-in-law said when I came back with the tea. "You really are an odd young woman. Interesting."

Maybe it was the loud volume that did the trick; at any rate, he left soon afterwards without attempting anything more than small talk. But that expression of his, "embracing water"....The words were etched on my mind for good. My carefree and convenient marriage was as fun as playing house, but it came with a price after all.

It was Sunday—and Christmas Eve no less—but Mutsuki was waxing the floor. I tried to help out by cleaning the windows, but Mutsuki told me not to bother. "Don't worry about it, I'll do it later," he said. Mutsuki always did the housecleaning on Sundays. It was one of his little hobbies.

"Shoko, why don't you go take a nap?" Mutsuki was obsessive about cleanliness. He wouldn't rest until everything in the house was clean and sparkling.

"Maybe I'll go polish the shoes then," I said, but Mutsuki had already done that too.

"What's the matter?" Mutsuki asked, quite puzzled, as I stood there at a loss for something to do. Sometimes he could be amazingly slow to catch on. But this was something we'd decided right from the start, that it didn't make any sense to say that a particular job was the husband's or the wife's. Whoever was better at it would be the one to do it, whether it was cleaning the house or cooking the meals or whatever.

I was feeling bored, so I got myself a bottle of white wine and went over to sit in front of the purple man. "Let's have a drink, shall we?" I said. "Just you and me. Forget boring old Mutsuki." The purple man looked delighted by the idea.

"Shoko." It came out sounding like a sigh. "You can't sit there. I'm trying to wax the floor."

I took a sip of the chilled German wine. "Grumpy Mutsuki." I had nowhere else to go. I escaped to the sofa and decided to sing the purple man a song. Bing Crosby's "White Christmas" was the one song I could sing in English. I sat there drinking my wine and singing my song. It was only a cheap wine, but it tasted nice and sweet. Mutsuki came over and took the bottle away.

"You're not supposed to drink it from the bottle, you know."

Suddenly I felt extremely unhappy. "Give it back," I said.

Mutsuki disappeared into the kitchen and put the wine in the refrigerator.

In protest, I started singing even louder, until my throat was sore and my eardrums started to hurt. But Mutsuki didn't relent a bit.

"Stop acting like a child," he said.

I felt like someone directly behind me was laughing at me, but when I turned around to look it was just Kon's tree, again. All of a sudden I lost my temper. I picked up the first things that came to hand—a duster and a bottle of cleaner—and hurled them at the tree. I was sick of it always looking at me like that.

"Shoko!" Mutsuki ran over and grabbed hold of me.

I felt unspeakably sad, and I started to cry out loud. There was nothing I could do; I couldn't control myself, and when I tried to stop crying I could hardly breathe. Mutsuki carried me over to my bed and told me to take it easy, that I'd feel much better if I had some sleep. But his kind words just annoyed me and made me feel even worse, and I continued to sob convulsively.

Eventually I fell asleep crying. By the time I woke up it was already evening. The apartment was spotless, there wasn't a speck of dust left anywhere.

"Why don't you take a bath?" Mutsuki suggested.

"Let's go out for dinner since it's Christmas," I said. Why did it always have to be like this? Mutsuki was so kind and sweet. It was kind of hard to take at times.

"Mutsuki?" Next year, I thought, I'll cook us something special.

"What?"

"Let's get a Christmas tree next year."

Mutsuki laughed, generous and warm and carefree as always. "Well, it's still this year, and here's your gift," he said, handing me a small package.

I untied the green ribbon and unwrapped the white paper. Inside was a small silver object shaped like a lily. It was too small and delicate to be an egg beater.

"It's a champagne stirrer," Mutsuki explained. It was for stirring up pretty little bubbles in your champagne.

"It's wonderful," I said. "Let's go out and get some really good champagne, and drink it tonight," I said, but Mutsuki shook his head.

"You don't need this for good champagne." A stirrer for making bubbles in cheap champagne. What a neat idea for a gift! I was impressed.

His first gift to me had been a teddy bear. It was a light pink color, a replica of an antique, and it came in a huge box wrapped in a ribbon. Mutsuki gave it to me the day after we first met.

The second was a globe made of transparent plastic. I fell in love with it the moment I saw it. I found it one day in a stationery shop where I was shopping for notebooks, and he bought it for me on the spot. He always knew what to get me.

"You like it?"

"Of course I do," I said. Then I remembered something.

Something terrible. It was Christmas, and I didn't have anything for Mutsuki. I hadn't even given it a thought.

"So what do you feel like eating?" he said.

"Um, Mutsuki? I got you a telescope, but because it's the end of the year and everything, they told me it might not get here on time...." I was surprised at how smoothly the lie came out.

"Wow!" Mutsuki's eyes shone. My husband was the sort of man who took people at their word.

How many couples would be having dinner out tonight, I wondered.

I could see the light of the room reflected in the freshly polished windows. There we all were: the purple man and Kon's tree; the gay husband and the alcoholic wife; all of us, glimmering faintly together in the windowpanes.

BLUE DEMON

• •

Shoko was still on the phone—unusual for her. True, she wasn't the one doing the talking, and she'd probably have hung up a while ago if she could have. Shoko hated the phone.

"You should call her," Kon used to tell me, and in the beginning I called Shoko pretty often. When I say in the beginning, I mean when I first met Shoko and we started seeing each other. Before we got married, obviously. According to Kon, all women were secret agents in the employ of the telephone company. But whenever I spoke to Shoko on the phone, she always sounded irritated.

"Maybe we should talk about this phone thing," she said one day.

"What phone thing?" I said, looking down at the ten-yen coin I was holding in my hand. It was a rainy night, and I was calling her from a phone in some bar with a Wild West theme.

"I mean, don't feel like you have to keep calling me all the time," she said. "Anyway, you don't really like talking on the phone either, do you, Mutsuki?"

I had to admit she was right. "No. How did you know?"

I looked over at Kon, who was sitting at the bar drinking with his back to me. I vowed then never to heed his theories about women again.

"Wanna drink?" A glass was thrust in front of my face. Shoko's long phone conversation had come to an end and I hadn't noticed.

"What's this?"

"It's called a Silver Streak—gin and kummel."

It was clear like sake. I took a sip just to be polite, and gave it back to Shoko. Receiving the glass, she savored a mouthful, swallowed it slowly, and smiled with contentment.

"Seems Mizuho is having mother-in-law problems."

"Oh?"

Mizuho was Shoko's best friend from high school. Her one and only friend, according to Shoko. Cheerful and lively, Mizuho was so wildly different from Shoko that the few times I had seen them together the strangeness of their attempts at communication had been pretty engrossing.

"I guess most mothers-in-law are impossible," Shoko said. Then she added, "In our case, she's really nice," with such sincerity that I felt a little bad.

At long last the gay son, who had happily vowed to die a bachelor, had come across a woman to his liking. It was only proper that his mother should be really nice to the woman for agreeing to a sexless union and becoming his wife. Shoko leaving me was my mother's idea of disaster.

"The business of medicine involves trust," my mother used to remind me. "Being single forever isn't good for your reputation."

Suddenly, a cushion came flying across the room and hit me in the face. I looked up to find Shoko sitting on the sofa, her lips drawn tightly together into a straight line.

"You're not listening."

Shoko's always quick to start throwing things around.

"Sorry. We were talking about Mizuho, right?"

"Yeah, and tomorrow I'm supposed to go over to her place. I might be a little late. Is that fine?"

I said it was fine. "Want me to pick you up around nine?"

Shoko shook her head and looked me straight in the eye. "Why don't you go see Kon for a change?" Her tone was serious, as if we were discussing something important. "I bet he really misses you."

It was a strange feeling, a wife worrying about her husband's lover.

"Uh-uh, Kon isn't the sort to feel lonely. But thanks for being so thoughtful."

"All right." Persuaded, Shoko smiled and finished off what was left of her cocktail.

My mother came to see me at the hospital the next day. I had just finished my morning rounds and was having a cup of coffee in the office.

"How is everything going?" she said.

A split second before I heard her voice behind me, I knew she was there. I recognized her perfume. "Hi, mom," I said. "You didn't need to come all this way. You should have stopped by the apartment." But I knew why she had come. She had something she wanted to discuss. Not with the two of us, but just with me. "How's dad?"

"Oh, he's fine." She took off her coat. She was wearing a white angora sweater, her full red lips blooming. She could have passed for ten years younger than her real age.

"How's Shoko?"

"Fine," I said, offering my mother a chair and a cup of coffee. I waited for her to get around to whatever it was she had come to say.

"The house is so empty without you," she said sadly. Her shoulders seemed to sag. "It's so cold this winter...."

"It *is* cold," I agreed. "There's something going around too, so be careful," I said.

"Is that so? Because my throat does feel a little sore. Do you have anything that might help?"

I could only laugh dryly at this. "I'm sure dad can give you something." My father was a doctor too, with his own practice. "What was it you really wanted to talk to me about?" I spoke first to help her along, since she seemed to be having so much trouble getting to the point. She lowered her voice, whispering her reply. "It's about having children."

"Children?"

My mother started to cross-examine me. "What do you think? Have you discussed it with Shoko?"

"We only got married last month."

"Mutsuki. Dr. Kakii is a gynecologist, isn't he?" my mother asked. Kakii was a friend of mine who worked at the same hospital. "Why don't you go in for a consultation—about artificial insemination?" My mother spoke the words as easily as if she were pronouncing the name of some dessert. Artificial insemination. Well, it had to be about something.

"Sorry to disappoint you, mom, but I haven't discussed anything of that sort with Shoko."

My mother's disappointment showed plainly on her face. "Well that's just not normal. No healthy woman would not care about such things," she said.

"I'll talk to her about it soon," I said, pressing the elevator button. "I'll let you know as soon as we come to any decision. If and when."

The cream-colored doors slid open, and I ushered my mother inside.

"Take care. Give dad my best. We'll come and visit soon. Shoko wants to see you again too."

My mother gave me a hard stare. "Mutsuki." Then came her trump card. "Don't forget, you're our only son."

The elevator doors slid shut before I could object. I stood there and watched the floor lamp until it indicated the ground lobby. I heaved a sigh.

I called Kon from the public phone near the elevator. He was still a student and spent most of his mornings asleep in his dorm. As I called I thought, "Funny Shoko told me to call him; I want to see him tonight like I haven't in a while."

I got home to find Shoko singing to herself again. Well, actually, not quite to herself. She was singing to the Cézanne watercolor on the wall. "Who's That Child?" seemed to be the song of the day. She's kind of strange like that sometimes, my wife.

"Hi, I'm home."

I loved the look on Shoko's face when she turned around to welcome me home. She was not someone who could ever fake cheerfulness. First a look of complete surprise spread over her features, as if to say, I never even dreamed you would come home, followed by a slow smile. Ah, now I remember, it seemed to say. Her reaction filled me with a sense of relief every time. This person was not counting the hours and minutes until I came home.

"How was Mizuho?" I asked, taking off my coat.

"Better than I thought she'd be."

"Well, that's good."

"I asked her to come over for the bean-throwing on Saturday. The husband and kid are coming too."

"Bean-throwing?"

"It's the first day of spring this Saturday," Shoko said. Traditional holidays that called for festive behavior were really big with Shoko. In fact, the only time I ever tasted her cuisine was when she made rice gruel with "the seven spring herbs" in accordance with the old calendar. Chopping and swiping clumsily at the herbs, she had told me that age-old customs were quite romantic in her opinion.

"That time of year already, huh?" I said.

"And you're playing the demon, okay?" This was spoken in a tone that left no room for discussion.

I was in the bath when Shoko came through the door, a glass of whiskey in her hand. She was still in her clothes.

"Tell me a story about Kon."

"What kind of story?" Nothing impeded my wife when she felt bored.

"Any kind."

I thought about it for a while, until I remembered a story that wouldn't take too long to tell. While I was in the tub, Shoko stood in the washing area; when I got out to rinse myself off, she sat on the edge of the tub, and listened quietly to my story.

"Few people love pranks more than Kon. And for him, friends aren't interesting targets. He has to choose a victim from the innocent general populace. He's got a whole variety of pranks, and they're all innocuous, but one that I really like is pulled off at the movies. He finds some place where they're showing a real tearjerker—say about parted lovers or a terminally ill little boy—and sits right next to someone he judges to be a big weeper at these things. It might be a college girl on a cute date with her cute boyfriend. It might be a young woman who's dressed like she might work at a day-care center. And then, just when she's about to start crying, when tears are beginning to fill her eyes, Kon sneezes. And it's a serious sneeze we're talking about. Aaagh-choof!! Like that. And the poor girl has lost her chance 'to let it all come out.' But she's not in any shape to laugh either. So she ends up with a runny nose and this amazing, contorted look on her face."

Suddenly I could picture it, and I started laughing. Kon was a prankster with true flair.

"Why would he want to do something like that?" Shoko's expression was stern.

"I don't know," I said. Kon hated pity and made fun of people who wept in public.

"That's the way he is," I said, rinsing myself off in the

shower. Kon had zero tolerance for people who never asked themselves if some of their own acts might not be more embarrassing than being gay.

There's nothing like a drink of Evian just after you get out of the bath. You can feel the pureness of the water spreading through your whole body. It makes me feel cleansed, purified, all the way to my fingertips. I went out on the veranda and gulped the water down noisily.

"I hate the bottles your Evian comes in," Shoko said. She was bundled up in a blanket, her hands wrapped around a hot glass of whiskey. "You want to share the blanket? You'll catch a chill if you're not careful."

"I'm fine," I said, "It feels good." I looked through the telescope. It was a gift from Shoko.

"The thing I don't like about Evian bottles is that weird flimsiness. It doesn't feel like a bottle at all."

I looked up through the telescope at a small, neatly trimmed patch of sky. Within my round, cut-out section of the universe, more stars than I could fathom were twinkling and shining. I rubbed my eyes, dazzled by the light of Rigel, reaching me from nine hundred light-years away, Procyon from eleven, and Capella from forty.

"Wanna look?"

Shoko shook her head. "Nah. As if I'm ever going to visit another galaxy. It doesn't interest me at all. I'll go heat up the bed for you," she said, and disappeared into the bedroom.

I liked watching Shoko's back while she ironed the sheets. It was weird. She took it so seriously. All she needed to do was warm up the bed a bit, but she insisted on ironing out every last crease and wrinkle she could find, until the whole bed looked incredibly crisp.

"Shoko."

"What," she said, smiling and tilting her head to one side.

"You remember what we decided when we got married?"

"What," Shoko said again. "We decided a lot of things. What are you talking about?"

"About lovers."

"You mean Kon?"

"No," I said. "I mean yours."

Her face clouded over. "If you're talking about Haneki, we broke things off completely. I've already told you that before."

"But we're supposed to be free to see other people. That's what we said when we got married."

"Just being with you is good enough for me, Mutsuki." She said this teasingly, and pulled the plug out of the outlet. "Go ahead, it's ready," she said, turning around to face me. "You can get into bed now."

I closed my eyes but couldn't fall asleep. I tossed and turned for a while but eventually gave up. When I opened my eyes and looked over at Shoko's bed, it was still untouched. I looked at the clock. It was past one already.

"You still up?" I hollered. I threw on a sweater and opened the bedroom door. Shoko was in the living room. I could feel the tension in the air, and I knew right away that she was feeling depressed. The bright light dazzled my eyes, and I blinked my way over to where Shoko was sitting on a cushion, hunched over a table, drawing something quietly and intently on a piece of paper.

"What are you doing?" I asked as casually as I could, and glanced over at the whiskey bottle. What had started off the night three-quarters full was now down to a third.

Shoko was making a demon mask. The blue demon on the paper had purple horns and a bright red mouth. She was just doing its thick black eyebrows when I looked.

"Wow. That's pretty good."

Shoko didn't respond. Her next move would be one of two things. Either she would throw something, or she would burst into tears.

Suddenly the hand holding the crayon stopped moving, and without a sound Shoko began to cry. Huge teardrops welled up in her eyes and rolled down her cheeks. From time to time, she let out a pained sob.

"Shoko."

Shoko covered her face with her hands and moaned quietly, and then started bawling like a child. She was saying something in between her sobs, but I couldn't make out what it was.

"I can't understand what you're saying, Shoko. Calm down and tell me slowly." There was nothing I could do but be patient and wait. I knew that trying to touch her or hug her would only make things worse. I crouched down beside her.

Shoko kept on crying for a very long time. In between sniffles and sobs I could make out a few words. She seemed to be accusing me of something. "Mutsuki...lovers..." But I couldn't make out what she was getting at. I practically dragged her into the bedroom and pushed her into bed.

"Good night."

Shoko was still looking at me accusingly with teary eyes. Her face was red and swollen.

I reached out a finger and touched her hot and puffy eyelid. "Okay. I won't talk about lovers, ever," I said sadly.

The bean-throwing party turned out to be a huge success. Mizuho was as lively and cheerful as ever, her bespectacled husband was pleasant and sensible throughout the occasion, and their young son Yuta looked rounder and chubbier every time I saw him. "How old are you now?" I asked him, and before I'd even finished my question, he held up three fat and stubby fingers in front of my face and waved them about clumsily in the air.

I put on the blue demon mask Shoko had made, and confronted the bean-throwers head-on, screaming and yelling and generally making a racket as I ran up and down the hallway trying to dodge the hard, uncooked beans. Everyone laughed at the way I struggled to avoid the missiles, but when they did hit me on the bony parts of my hands and head, it really hurt. "Out with the demon! Out with the demon!" they all shouted; I couldn't help noticing that Shoko was the one with the most determined look on her face.

After the bean-throwing, we sat down for some beer. Shoko insisted that we all eat the number of beans corresponding to our ages, so we counted them out, one by one, and made sure that everyone ate the right amount, like it or not. No doubt when we were eighty Shoko would insist on eating exactly eighty beans. As I chewed on my beans, I tried to picture Shoko at eighty, wrinkled and frail.

It was a strange feeling. Suddenly our inanimate little apartment was alive with human energy, and Shoko and I were both starting to feel a bit restless and uncomfortable. It was creepy to think that all the energy and vitality was coming from one, small family: Yuta bouncing up and down on the sofa and rattling the blinds open and shut, his young parents following him carefully out of the corner of their eyes, ready to leap up and bring him under control the moment he got out of hand. We sat and watched the toons on TV with the kid, ate delivery sushi, and drank our beer.

"Children are such troublesome creatures," Shoko said with great feeling as she poured cold tea into the potted plant Kon had given us. Shoko was convinced that the plant relished the tea she kept feeding it. She claimed the tree shook its leaves with pleasure whenever she gave it tea.

"Ten o'clock already, huh?" she said.

Ten o'clock. It was around eight-thirty when our guests had finally gone clattering out of the apartment, so Shoko must have been sitting there glaring at the plant for nearly an hour and a half now.

"How long are you going to keep sitting there like that?" I was about to ask her, but she beat me to it.

"Mutsuki, do you realize you've been cleaning the apartment for an hour and a half now?"

"But there're fingerprints and stains everywhere—on the tables, the windows, the TV, all over the floor...on the phone...."

Shoko was giving me a strange look. "But you've been at it ever since they left. It's not normal."

But you've been at it ever since they left, it's not normal, I repeated after her silently.

"We make a pretty good couple, you know, you and me. Like two peas in a pod."

"What's that supposed to mean?" said Shoko. "I don't think we're alike at all."

"You want a drink?" I asked.

"Hmm—a double," she said.

I got a bottle and some cucumbers and went out onto the veranda. I decided not to mention the conversation I'd had with my mother.

"You want some cheese?" Shoko shouted from the kitchen.

"Sounds good," I called back, looking out across the vast fabric of the night-time sky. I bit into a cucumber and felt its fresh taste fill my mouth as I looked up at the stars.

MONOCEROS: THE UNICORN

• •

I had a dream about an old boyfriend of mine. He looked the same as ever, his eyebrows knit together and a sad, serious look on his face. He had on an oversized gray sweater he often used to wear back in college, and he was carrying a bunch of white freesias in his hands.

"Shoko-chan," he said. (He always said my name really mechanically.) "I can't go on without you." The furrow between his brows deepened. "I'm sorry I said such horrible things," he mumbled, biting his bottom lip. "Look, Shoko-chan, I brought you your favorite flowers, and some of those cream puffs you like so much."

Mini cream puffs, from Morozoff, I thought to myself in my dream. "What flavor are they?" I asked.

My old boyfriend smiled brightly. "Your favorite, of course: cointreau."

Cointreau-flavor cream puffs! Suddenly, I felt a whole lot better about everything.

It was nine-fifteen when I woke up, and Mutsuki was already gone. When I wandered into the living room in my pajamas I could smell coffee. The living room looked spick-and-span as always, and the heater was clanking away in the corner. I pressed the play button on the multi-disc CD player, and soft low-volume music began to filter through the room. Suddenly, I became uneasy. I felt as though Mutsuki was never going to come home again. Maybe he had never existed to begin with. The room seemed unnaturally bright. The background music sounded morbidly clear. Nothing felt real.

I was desperate to hear Mutsuki's voice again. It was all his fault that I had that dream about Haneki. Mutsuki was the one who had brought up the subject. All the worry and fear I had been keeping bottled up inside of me came gushing up my throat, and I could feel myself on the verge of tears.

"Hello?" A woman picked up on the second ring. She spoke the name of the hospital in a cold, distant voice.

"I'd like to speak to Mutsuki Kishida, internal medicine, please."

"One moment please."

She put me on hold, and "O Vreneli" came on in the background. I felt as though someone was making fun of me. Then the music stopped and the woman's voice came back on. "I'm sorry, he hasn't come in yet."

I got dressed hurriedly and grabbed my purse, and then went out. I could feel the sunshine and the dust in the air. I had to take three different buses before I got to the hospital. (Actually you were only supposed to have to change once, but the bus routes and timetables were so complicated that it was impossible to get the transfers right.) I looked out the window and watched the scenery crawl by. A few family restaurants, a cabbage patch, and then a mayonnaise factory.

Haneki and I broke up not long before I was due to be introduced to Mutsuki. Let's not see each other anymore, he'd said desolately. (Actually that's the way he looked all of the time. I used to love the cloud of sadness that seemed to brood over his forehead.)

"You're not normal, Shoko-chan," he said. "Men are social creatures. Your wildness is one of the things that appeals to me about you, but beyond a certain point, I just can't keep up with you. It's my fault, really."

I still don't have a clue what he was trying to say.

"I'm sorry." I remember the way his forehead looked as he bowed his head, pain and suffering carved into the creases between his brows.

The hospital was a huge red-brick building. I asked the nurse at reception for directions to the doctors' offices. She picked up the phone without even looking at me. "One moment, please," she said. And then, "Name please?"

"Shoko Kishida," I told her. The nurse gave me a quick look up and down and flashed me a ridiculously overdone grin. She pointed to the sofa and told me to have a seat.

I felt sick. I sat down on the synthetic green sofa and stared blankly at the dimly lit lobby. Old-fashioned stained glass windows, people sitting around waiting with dull stagnant looks, and a bright shiny vending machine that looked like it had found its way here by mistake. There was a humid sickly smell of plants, and a giant oversized oil painting that was enough to make anybody feel ill. And this was where Mutsuki worked.

"Shoko?" Suddenly, there he was in front of me, with his beautiful clear eyes, and his soft wavy hair: my beloved Mutsuki. "What's up? You've never come here before."

I stood up. I wanted to tell Mutsuki everything: the dream about Haneki, the way I'd suddenly been so desperate to come and see him, about how I got all confused with the buses, how the nurse had been mean to me, how lonely and uneasy I'd felt waiting for him in the lobby.... But I didn't know where to start.

"Uh, Shoko?"

"I want to go home," I managed to say at last. But this didn't seem to strike Mutsuki as sensible.

"I'm going home because I want to go home." I felt better now that I'd seen his face and somehow managed to elaborate that much.

"Well, I guess I won't keep you," Mutsuki said. He sounded a bit confused.

"Hey, is she your wife?" I heard someone bellow behind me. When I turned around, I saw a short man in thick glasses with black frames, with reddish skin that made him look as though he had just stepped out of the bath. How handsome Mutsuki looks in his regulation white next to this guy, I thought.

"I'm Kakii. Gynecology. We spoke once on the phone, I think. I'm a friend of Mutsuki's from college."

I didn't remember ever speaking to him, but I smiled anyway and said hello.

"Well, what a surprise. I never expected to see you here," he said, a little too loudly. "He's so secretive! He could have introduced us before you got married, at least. We go way back, you know. We tackled the state exams together as students."

"Ah." I didn't know what to say. As a matter of fact, I had never met any of Mutsuki's friends. We didn't have a wedding reception or anything, true, but our not having met was a bit strange indeed. I'd never even come to see Mutsuki at the hospital yet.

"Dr. Kakii?"

"Yes?" This guy smiled a lot.

"Nice to meet you at last," I said, "and I do hope you'll come over and see us before long." I was starting to feel like a real doctor's wife. I could see Mutsuki was ready to sigh.

Outside, on the other side of the automatic doors, I could see bright rays of sunshine.

"Okay, take care getting home then. And don't forget, you have to take the #6 bus and change to #1 when you see the big office building."

"Okay. Thanks," I said as I started off down the stone steps.

"You sure there wasn't something you wanted to talk about?" Mutsuki called after me. I waved my hand as I walked away to say, "Nope—nothing at all."

After my bath, I got out a can of tomato juice from the refrigerator and took a sip.

"When should we have people over?" I asked, slicing up a baguette. Mutsuki was stirring the stew.

"Not for a while yet, I think," he said.

"Why not?"

"I don't know. Just because."

"Don't you like Dr. Kakii?" I asked, nibbling at the slice I had just buttered.

"I like him. He's a nice guy."

"Oh yeah?" Then, I thought, there's only one possible reason he's reluctant to invite anyone over. Mutsuki doesn't want any of his friends to meet me. "Let me know when the stew's ready," I said. I went into the living room and fed what was left of my tomato juice to Kon's tree.

"Here, try this," I said. "It tastes like blood."

It made sense, I supposed. An emotionally unstable, alcoholic wife wasn't really something you wanted to show off to the whole world.

"You sure it's okay giving it tomato juice like that?" Mutsuki said from the kitchen.

"It's good for it. Full of nutrition." I put some ice in a glass and poured vodka over it, and then mixed it with kahlua. The inky dark liquid looked like poison, and it suited my mood perfectly. I took a book of poetry down from Mutsuki's bookshelf and flipped through it. It wasn't in the least bit interesting.

"Tell me more about Kon," I shouted in the direction of the kitchen. There was silence for a while. Finally, he asked back, "What kind of story would you like?"

"Tell me about when you have sex."

There was no reply. I shouted out the same words and Mutsuki came out into the living room, a wooden spoon still in his hand. "What's wrong? You're in a bad mood," he said quietly.

"Tell me about when you and Kon have sex."

"Okay," he said with a grin. For a while he looked as if he were really thinking about it. "Well, let me see…he has a really straight back and…and he smells like coke."

I was looking straight ahead, at the side of Mutsuki's face.

"He has a tan the whole year round, and he's got narrow hips. And, well…yeah, his hips smell like coke, too."

Like coke? And then he mumbled something under his breath that sounded like "and that's all." Before I could complain, he disappeared into the kitchen to check on the stew.

Dinner was over in no time. Neither of us spoke a word.

"Hey." Mutsuki was having a cup of coffee in the living room. Suddenly he got up and moved a book around on his shelf.

"What's the matter?"

"Nothing," he said, and smiled at me gently.

"What do you mean, nothing?" I said, annoyed. "That was the book I was just reading, right? If you want to tell me not to touch your books, or to ask you first, why don't you just go ahead and speak up instead of pretending like it doesn't matter?"

"All right—you got me there," Mutsuki admitted. "But you're allowed to read whatever you want. It's just that I have a system. Here, let me show you. It's pretty simple. All the French poetry goes here. Alain Bousquet, André Breton, Raymond Queneau.... Spanish poetry comes over here. Well, I only have this one Lorca, but anyway.... There's the Italian poetry, and there's the German poetry...."

"Okay, that's enough, I get the idea," I said. "And then when you take one off the shelf, you put a little marker in its place to mark the spot, right?"

"Hey, that's not a bad idea," Mutsuki said.

It annoyed me that Mutsuki didn't seem to notice the sarcastic nature of my suggestion. "I guess it's not surprising you don't invite people over, is it, when your wife can't even manage to keep your books in order on the shelf...."

"Shoko," Mutsuki sighed. It always made me sad when Mutsuki looked me straight in the eye like that. I always had to look away when he fixed those kind eyes of his on me.

"You know, Kakii...." Mutsuki said as he set up his telescope on the veranda. "Kakii isn't...normal either. It's quite common among doctors, actually."

At first, I didn't understand what he meant by "not normal."

"I think he regards marriage as immoral for our sort. That's why he's so interested in us, you see. He's curious what kind of lifestyle our immoral deed might have gotten us into."

"Is Dr. Kakii gay?"

Mutsuki laughed at my astonishment. "Well, to tell you the truth...there's quite a lot of us around, you know."

And then he told me a little more about what it was like to be gay, as he stood there looking up through the telescope at the stars. The various types of gay men he knew, and the kinds of things they went through. "Everyone's different, though, you know. Especially since so many people never come out of the closet. And then there's latent homosexuality, or whatever it's called. You can't categorize people so easily. Not like books on a shelf."

I went and got myself some whiskey and sat taking small sips of it as I listened.

"Kakii is what Kon calls a dime-novel queer," Mutsuki said. "He comes from a gynecologist household, and he's felt awe and fear for the female body ever since he was a kid. Add to that this huge complex he's got over his looks, and what do you get? It's so clichéd."

"Yup," I said. So that's how it happens, I was thinking to myself.

"And what triggered it all is this teacher he had in high school. Again, same old story."

I said nothing. So there was always something that triggered it?

"And what makes it even more like something out of a cheap novel is that his boyfriend is the 'narcissistic, beautiful youth' type," Mutsuki said, with what sounded like scornful laughter. "But I guess we all have a cheap novel in us somewhere."

"What was it that did it in your case?"

"Kon," he said simply, stepping away from the telescope. "You want to have a look?" he asked. "You can see Monoceros."

I wondered what exactly that meant, Kon starting it all off. I looked through the telescope, but I couldn't figure out any Monoceros.

"So many stars!"

"Amazing, isn't it," Mutsuki said.

"It looks so different through the telescope." It was as if someone had inlaid the whole of the sky with millions of tiny glittering jewels.

"You can see a lot more in the country. Even with the naked eye."

It's not right, I thought. It was the city sky that needed more stars, just as it was people like Mutsuki who were the most in need of a woman. Not a woman like me—someone nicer, less messed-up.

"I had a dream about Haneki this morning," I said.

"What kind of dream?"

"A really nice one."

Mutsuki laughed.

"But it's not my fault," I said. "It's your fault. You were the one who brought up boyfriends."

"You need a boyfriend too, Shoko."

I said I didn't want one, and Mutsuki looked really sad.

"But I can't do anything for you."

I didn't say anything. "Let's invite Dr. Kakii over. And Dr. Kakii's boyfriend. And Kon, too. We can have a little party."

Mutsuki was silent.

"And hey, next time you feel like buying me something," I said, "get me some cream puffs. The ones from Morozoff. Cointreau flavor."

"I'll buy some tomorrow," Mutsuki said, and laughed a laugh

that was pure, innocent, and carefree.

I dragged Kon's tree out onto the veranda with us. It looked like it was enjoying the night breeze sweeping over its leaves.

"'Night." I went inside first, thinking that Mutsuki might want some time to himself. I ironed his bed. It was fine to have marriages like ours. You didn't expect much, you didn't wish for much. You didn't lose anything, there was nothing to be afraid of. Suddenly, I remembered my father-in-law's words. Embracing water.

"It's ready!" I shouted. I pulled the blanket back over the bed and pulled the plug out of the outlet. I closed my eyes and breathed in slowly. In the dark, a star-filled sky rolled open like a bed of jewels.

THE VISITORS, THE SLEEPERS, AND ONE THAT WATCHETH

• •

"You'll burn a hole in your stomach, drinking all that coffee," the nurse said.

"Right, thanks for the warning," I said, pouring out my fifth cup. Just thinking about the night ahead was enough to give me ulcers.

Kon's stubbornness exasperated me. I was practically begging him, but he didn't budge an inch. All I was asking him to do was to pretend he couldn't make the party.

"Mm-hmm," Kon's voice came through the receiver. Laughter. "You want me to stay away that bad, huh?"

"Don't get me wrong. It's partly that Kakii and others are coming too. You never liked them much."

"Oh yeah?"

"We'll have you over some other time. I promise."

"Being married is no laughing matter," Kon threw out as casually as ever, "but I don't like this." Weren't we the ones who had invited him, after all?

"I know. That's why I'm begging you."

Kon's face was aglow. I didn't need to see him to tell, the phone line could not but transmit such smugness.

"I'm not coming if you don't want me to, but make sure your wife knows exactly why. Some misgiving of yours, not mine, will be responsible for my absence." Kon was clearly enjoying himself.

"Seven o'clock, right?" He told me to say my prayers, had a good laugh, and hung up.

Shoko had been in unusually high spirits when I left home that morning. "I'll get us some *inari* sushi and sushi rolls and chips and veggies and ice cream, so can you pick up fried chicken on your way home? That should be enough."

"Sounds like the menu for a kid's birthday party."

Shoko agreed and laughed happily. "Tonight at seven," she double-checked for one last time as she walked me to the door.

"Oh, and..." she added, her voice suddenly flat, "I'll be ready to go out on a moment's notice if and when you feel like it. Don't worry about that."

"About what?" It took me three seconds to get it. "Give me a break, Shoko, and don't be so absurd." It was too much. Homosexuality was mixed up in her mind with perversion.

"We're not sex maniacs, you know," I explained, weirdly flustered. Having to spell things out was nearly making me blush. "Listen, Shoko. A few friends are getting together for dinner, that's all. You don't have to concern yourself with anything like that."

Her thin eyebrows knit close, she heard this out meekly.

"Now I see," she said, and nodded slowly, as to a profound thought.

I stopped by Meiji-ya for some fried chicken and picked up Kashibe at Hiro-o intersection. A brain surgeon who worked at a general hospital in the neighborhood, Kashibe was Kakii's boyfriend. Pale, thin, quiet, and handsome, he was said to be in his late thirties but looked more like twenty-seven or thereabouts.

"Are you sure I can come too?" Kashibe asked as he got into the car.

Sitting shotgun was Kakii, the last person a driver would ever want there. Not happy with merely fidgeting, Kakii made infuriating clinking noises with the seat belt once every three minutes, buckling or unbuckling. The radio he tuned constantly, changing stations as soon as a song ended. Adding to all the noise was his running commentary—telling me not to drive too close, making sure I had seen a speed limit sign.

"Maybe I'll bring her a cake instead of flowers," he said, biting on his nails. "Is the woman a sweet-tooth?"

"She is." I didn't like the way he said "the woman." It was vulgar. "You're not spitting out that bit of nail in my car."

"'Course not," Kakii said and opened the window. His face

turned red. Kakii was easily flustered, and blushed immediately when he was.

"Is there a bakery near your place?" He spat the chewed bit of nail out the window.

"Yeah."

"Can we stop by on the way? Watch, light's gonna change."

I know, I told him.

We arrived home to find some guests had arrived early: Shoko's parents, and Kon. The idea of them bunched together— it gave me a chill.

"You're late!" Shoko accused. The clock told seven sharp.

You're late, you're late, you're late, she muttered the words over and over like a chant, glaring hard at me and the freshly arrived guests. Kakii and Kashibe quailed at this.

"Sorry we arrived early!" Shoko's mother piped.

I could feel Kakii tense up next to me and blush to the tips of his ears. Whenever Kakii was confronted with an "older person" (that's to say, anybody above forty leading a standard family life), he felt intimidated and clammed up.

"Man, he's autistic."

The remark was Kon's, who continued, "So I guess seven was it, huh? I don't know how I got that wrong!" The brazen liar laughed innocently. "I could have sworn we had said five."

I was aghast. The smell of hot fried chicken was meeting Shoko's mother's perfume in our cramped two bedroom apartment. I felt suffocated. Chaos was in the air.

"Mutsuki tells me you have a sweet tooth," Kashibe practically whispered, as he handed Shoko the cake box.

"Oh, thank you! You're so thoughtful." It wasn't Shoko, but her mother who said this. I felt weak.

"Well, what a gathering," said Shoko's father. Why was everyone being so jolly? "All doctors, are you?"

I made the necessary introductions.

"Kon's been telling everyone all about you, Mutsuki," Shoko said. My fingers tingled, and I broke into a cold sweat.

"Very nice, very nice!" said Shoko's father, thumping me on the shoulders, leaving me to wonder what was so very nice. Then he got up and said, "Well, I guess we'd better be on our way, then."

My mother-in-law looked as though she wanted to stay a little longer, but Shoko went and got her coat, so she had no choice but to get up too.

We all got up to see them to the door. Kon saw them off with more warmth and energy than anybody else, but when we got back to the living room, he was the one who murmured, "Well, now we can breathe easy at last."

"Sit anywhere," I said, clearing away the tea things. Shoko was pouring the leftover tea into the potted plant.

"Nice place you got here." Kakii was back to his usual cheerful self. So this is the bedroom, right, and this must be the

bathroom, he said, looking around the apartment before set-
tling on the sofa. "Very nice, very nice."

Shoko had made mint juleps, and she set one down in front
of each of us. She placed a bottle of bourbon in the middle of
the table. "Help yourselves!"

It really did feel like a children's party, what with the sushi
and the fried chicken all lined up on the table. And then Shoko
brought in a huge basket overflowing with raw vegetables, and
everyone's mouth dropped open. The carrots and radishes, at
least, had been cut into chunks, very large chunks, but the
cucumbers and lettuce hadn't been touched at all. She had
rinsed them under the faucet just before carrying them in, and
they were still dripping with water.

"Well, don't you feel like snacking on vegetables when
you're drinking?" she said, by way of excuse. I took a closer look
and noticed that the basket she was serving the vegetables in
was actually the kitchen strainer.

Normally Kon would have smiled disdainfully at this kind of
behavior, but tonight he was the first to start eating. He bit into
what looked like a particularly tough carrot, munching on it
noisily, as Shoko launched herself into a stick of celery. Quietly,
the rest of us followed their lead. A bizarre scene. I picked off
two or three lettuce leaves and nibbled at them slowly. They
hardly tasted of anything at all.

"You're right to listen to what your body tells you, Shoko,"

Kashibe said, much to everybody's surprise. He hardly ever spoke unless spoken to. "Alcohol causes the body to produce a lot of acid. Vegetables are good for you, especially when you're drinking."

For the first time that evening, Shoko was smiling with what looked like real happiness.

It was a strange evening. I don't know about Kashibe, but Kakii and I usually never drank very much. Kon wasn't a big drinker either, but that night, we all gulped down the mint juleps. It's a sweet drink, much stronger than it tastes, and it really gets the appetite going. We drank a lot, and ate a lot, and talked a lot. All the worries, the anxieties, that had been nagging me all day: that Kon would act like his usual self, taking jabs at Shoko; that Shoko would become morose or lose her temper; that Kakii would poke fun at our marriage—or at Shoko, for that matter—and study us both with that morbid curiosity of his: the million or more misgivings I'd had about the party turned out to have been nothing more than imaginary fears. In fact, I had to admit that the apartment felt brighter, more cheerful, and more comfortable that night than ever before.

Kon didn't put out his claws even once. We were like a group of dorm students out of some TV sit-com. Even Kakii had managed to shake off his usual nervousness and seemed relaxed and at ease. Kashibe didn't say much, but he clearly liked Shoko, and he gave every sign of enjoying being part of the unlikely assembly. As for Shoko, she drank at her usual relentless pace but managed to keep her temper under control in a way that astonished me. She did keep breaking into song from time to time, and at one stage took the oil painting off the wall and put it down next to her; apart from that there was nothing really unusual about her behavior at all. She came across as more bright and cheerful than anything else.

"I guess I'd better get going if I'm going to make the last train."

It's hard to describe the atmosphere that descended upon the room when Kon spoke those words. It was as though we were kids suddenly forced to stop playing in the middle of a favorite game. There was a moment of awkwardness and embarrassment, and then an overwhelming surge of surprise and confusion that we had been feeling that way. We actually had to come back to reality.

"But there's still the ice cream," Shoko said. Too late. We were back in reality.

No one wanted any dessert, and the curtain finally fell on the evening that we had felt could go on forever. Slowly we started to make our way toward the door.

It took about thirteen minutes to get to the station from our place, and it was easy to get lost if you didn't know the way, but Kon said he'd be fine on his own. And he was probably right; he had an uncanny sense of direction and sharply honed animal instincts. But Shoko wouldn't take no for an answer, and we all set off together, wandering through the quiet night-time streets in the direction of the station. We walked in silence. No one said a thing, but it wasn't awkward or strained—it was more comical than anything. We shuffled quietly through the silent streets, Shoko at our side spooning ice cream into her mouth straight from the carton. We wound our way through deserted residential neighborhoods, not a soul in sight, the spring night warm and soft like chocolate cake.

It was Kon who broke the silence, as usual. We had made it as far as the little line of shops in front of the station when he stopped still.

"Actually, I think I'm gonna visit a friend," he said. "He lives right around here."

This was the first I'd ever heard of him.

"Where exactly?"

"Oh, just behind the Moriguchi tofu shop."

I'd never seen or heard of any such place, of course, but I knew it was useless to press him any further.

"Thank you for having me, *Shoko-chan*," he said, and then turned to leave.

Shoko stood and waved goodbye, as Kon's receding form wandered off into the night.

We made sure that Kakii and Kashibe made the last train, and then started back. The streets were filled with throngs of people just off the last train, all hurrying home.

On our way home we passed several convenience stores. Their doors slid open and shut as we went by, the smell of *oden* and Chinese dumplings drifting from the brightly-lit interiors onto the streets outside.

"Kon's so silly," Shoko said with a laugh. "As if they still have things like tofu shops these days."

"Yeah," I agreed. What was he thinking anyway, missing the last train home? I couldn't imagine a hard-up student like him taking a taxi.

"Here," said Shoko, handing me the ice cream.

"You don't want any more?"

"I'm offering to share it with you," Shoko said. She sounded disappointed. Most likely her hands were just getting cold from holding it so long.

"Thanks." I took the container from her. Shoko stuck her hands in the pockets of her skirt and ran through her impressions of the day, bubbling over with excitement. "They're all so nice," she said. "Especially Kon. You know what surprised me? They don't really seem effeminate, do they, though they're all gay?" (Shoko seemed to expect all gay men to prance around like beauty queens.) "And what about Dr. Kakii," she continued. "Weird or what, huh? He really bites his nails down to the quick."

"And then there's Dr. Kashibe," Shoko narrowed her eyes. "He kind of reminds me of a Kannon bodhisattva."

I had no idea what she meant by this strange metaphor, and was about to get her to explain, when suddenly she grabbed hold of my arm.

"Look!" I followed her eyes to a big house with a heavy, forbidding gate. Just beyond which, in the small pool of light by the gatepost, was a doghouse. And jutting out from inside the doghouse I could see a pair of jean-clad legs. I knew right away who it was.

"Kon!" We called out to him through the gate, and a dog started barking from inside the doghouse. The two legs scrambled to get free, and Kon's back emerged, followed by his shoulders and head.

"I almost had him then," he said. "And then you guys come along and get him all excited."

"What were you doing?"

The dog came flying out after Kon, straining at its leash and barking like crazy. Kon jumped the gate and came down next to us. "I feel like a burglar or something," he said.

The dog was still yapping away like mad, desperately trying to get close enough to sink its teeth into one of us. Any second now, the owner of the house was going to come rushing out to see what all the noise was about. We made a run for it, like real thieves. I had the ice cream in my right hand, and was holding

Shoko's hand in my left. As we ran, I could feel the mood of silliness and light-heartedness return. We ran until we couldn't hear the barking anymore and finally came to a halt. I looked over at Shoko trying to catch her breath, and saw that she was holding Kon's right hand in her left. Kon looked at me and smirked.

"Mutsuki, ice cream." Shoko gasped, breathing hard. I handed her the crushed container. The ice cream had melted, and it was all lumpy and runny inside ("Like a McShake," said Shoko).

"What the hell was that about?" I tried asking Kon again. "That was the friend you wanted to see?"

"Asshole," he said. "I was negotiating with it. Trying to get it to let me sleep over. And guess what? Turns out the dog's gay, too."

"Really?" Shoko asked, surprised. Kon nodded seriously.

"Kon!" I said, but he just smirked at me again.

Ridiculously enough, the three of us ended up spending the night together on the floor. At first Shoko insisted that she take the sofa and that "the two lovebirds" sleep in the bedroom. Naturally, I turned down her offer right away, but Kon, typical Kon, insisted on making things difficult, shrugging his shoulders and saying he didn't care where he slept, or with whom he slept. And so in the end, we reached a compromise and decided that we'd all sleep together on the living room floor.

"Feels like we're on a school trip," Shoko said. "Anyway, it's a nice change. Kind of fun."

I knew there was no way I could fall asleep like that. I can't even sleep in a strange bed. I was accustomed to freshly ironed sheets and a fresh warm blanket. My body knew every lump in the mattress. How was I supposed to be able to sleep like that, on a blanket spread out on the floor? And as if that wasn't enough, there I was with Shoko on my left, and Kon on my right.

"Mom and Dad were both so happy," Shoko said. "They both really liked Kon."

"Yeah?"

"He kept saying such nice things about you. My dad looked so proud. Like you're way too good for me."

Shoko was in a talkative mood. I could just picture Kon getting carried away, making up stories about me. I recalled my father-in-law's generous, understanding face and felt sad. How would he look if he could see us now, I wondered, his daughter, his son-in-law, and his son-in-law's boyfriend all snuggled up on the floor together like the Roman numeral III?

"You *are* too good for me, Mutsuki," Shoko said. "But you lost a point today. You were late. *Really* late. I waited five hours for you. Maybe even six."

"Oh, come on." It was surely hyperbole. Her parents' early

arrival must have been really taxing.

"I can feel rain!" Shoko jumped up and ran over to the window. "See, what did I tell you? It is raining! It was so humid, I knew it was going to rain."

She went into the kitchen, and I heard her open a can of beer. "You want one?" she asked.

"No thanks, I've had enough."

"What about Kon?" When there was no answer, she asked again. "What about Kon?"

"He's asleep." I looked over at his face as he slept, so peaceful and calm, and couldn't help smiling to myself. I mean, really. What was it like inside that head of his?

Shoko was standing by the window guzzling her beer. I could smell the rain coming in on the breeze.

A HANDFUL OF CANDY

· ·

Mutsuki's friends came over quite often after that. (Dr. Kakii and Dr. Kashibe only ever came at night, when Mutsuki was sure to be home, but Kon always came in the afternoon, when Mutsuki wasn't around.) They all like you a lot, Mutsuki told me. I liked them, too, so I was happy to hear that. Mutsuki was still as kind to me as ever, and four months into our marriage— eight since we'd first met—we still hadn't had a single real fight. What's the phrase they use, "smooth sailing"? Well, that's what it was. But even so, for some reason I seemed to be in a really bad mood all the time. I couldn't tell you why myself.

I was always being mean to Mutsuki. Once a day at least I'd say something hurtful, something bitchy, maybe a sarcastic joke. Winter gave way to spring, and soon it was May, but my mean moods just kept getting worse. It was almost as though nice weather fouled up my mood. I was at my worst on beautiful spring days, when a fresh breeze blew. May has always been a difficult month for me. Suddenly there's brightness and color everywhere, and the whole world's waking up and bursting back into life again. Inside the apartment too, Kon's tree was getting bigger and stronger every day.

"You busy with work or something these days?" Mutsuki said to me one morning. I wasn't. I asked him why he asked. He leaned his head slightly to one side. "You just seem a bit tired lately, that's all," he said.

He put on his shoes and dropped the key into his pocket, and opened the front door. "I'm on the night shift tonight, so don't forget to lock up. And remember to turn off the gas. And try not to let work pile up, okay?"

"Good. I'm glad. It seems like forever since you were on the night shift," I said. He gave me a confused-looking smile, and shut the door firmly behind him.

It was true that I didn't really mind when Mutsuki had to work nights. I find it easier to relax when I'm on my own. I like Mutsuki a lot, don't get me wrong; that's why I married him. I just don't believe in that kind of love where you've got to be with the person twenty-four seven. But still, I didn't really mean to say such a horrible thing to Mutsuki. The second the words came out of my mouth, I felt so sad I wanted to cry. What was wrong with me?

Mizuho told me once that the one complaint she had about her husband was that he was always going away on business. Every time he left town, she used to call me on the phone.

"We've only just got married, and already he's going off leaving me behind," she'd complain. "I don't know why we got married at all if it was going to be like this."

"Makes sense," I said (not very helpfully). "Who needs bait once you've caught the fish, right?"

"It's not like that at all," she said, not missing a beat. "He really misses me too, I know he does." Now she was contradicting herself. "You just don't understand, Shoko." She sounded kind of pissed. I just didn't understand. Come to think of it, maybe that's why I don't get so many calls from her like that anymore.

I snapped the dictionary shut, turned off the lamp, and got up from the desk. I couldn't concentrate on my work that night. I couldn't relax, even though I was alone. I poured myself some whiskey and went into the bathroom. I put the plug in the tub and turned on the tap. I watched the hot water gush into the tub and touched the tip of my tongue to my whiskey. Tiny waves rippled across the surface. I looked down at the ripples, keeping an ear out for the phone. I didn't want to miss my call.

I put my glass on top of the wash basin and went to get a pair of pajamas and some fresh underwear from the bedroom. I put them into my little basket, and went back to check on the bath. The tub was still only halfway full, so I went back into the living room and sang a few songs for the purple man. By the time I'd finished singing ("Rain," "The Orange Blossom Song" and a pop song by Kyon Kyon) the tub was eight-tenths full. I climbed in with my glass of whiskey. I dragged the phone into the bathroom with me, and put it in the changing area on top of my pajamas.

It felt like ages since the last time I'd been able to drink whiskey in the bath. Mutsuki had forbidden it. Before I got married I often used to soak in the tub with a glass of whiskey. It's a great feeling. The alcohol goes straight to your head, and you can feel it working its magic as it courses its way through your system. I used to love it. I could feel all the blood in my body fizzing like soda water, shooting through my veins like the jet-stream in a water slide. My head swimming, my senses strangely acute.

Mutsuki said it was really bad for your heart. He made me promise not to do it again. Ever. I nodded, and told him I never would, but I didn't really mean it. I slapped at the surface of the water now, making little splashing noises. I didn't think anything of lying. In fact, I was surprised I'd managed to keep my promise for four long months. I slapped at the water some more with my hands. The water splashed and sloshed over the sides of the tub, until my hands turned numb.

I got out of the tub and drank a mini-sized can of beer. I could feel the whiskey mixing with the beer behind my eyes. Waves of drunkenness washed over me, and I felt dizzy.

The phone never rang.

When Mutsuki came home, he had a whole bunch of donuts with him as usual. Doctors who worked nights at the hospital always got the whole of the next morning off. Since they were back on call in the afternoon, it would have made more sense to stay and rest at the hospital, but Mutsuki always came home. He would stop to buy some donuts on his way, and we would have breakfast together, and then he would take a shower, change into a clean shirt, and head back to the hospital. A fresh start every day, that was Mutsuki's policy.

"It's really nice out," he said, brushing the lint off the suit he had just changed out of.

"I know. We have windows, you know."

Mutsuki stopped and glanced over at me. And then, in a bright cheerful voice, he said, "They had a new kind of donut. Guess what it was."

"Dunno...."

"Plain raisin," he said. "Open it and see." He gestured with his chin toward the box on the table. "Remember you said something once about raisin donuts always coming with that cinnamon flavor? Because you like raisins but not cinnamon? Well, these ones are plain, so I thought you'd like them—"

"Mutsuki," I interrupted. I couldn't take it any more. Why did he have to be so *nice* all the time? In my heart, I was pleading with him to stop talking, but obviously he couldn't hear me.

"I asked the girl in the shop, you know, just to make sure. She was really nice. She even gave me a free sample—"

"Okay, that's enough." Talking about donuts the minute he gets home. It was giving me heartburn.

"Shoko, what are you so mad about?" he asked. Mutsuki thought there had to be a reason for everything.

"I'm not mad. I'm just not hungry. You didn't have to get me anything. Don't you get tired after working all night? You didn't have to come home, you know," I rattled on.

I said I was going to take a nap and went back to bed. I buried myself under the sheets and cried. I couldn't control myself any longer. I tried to stifle my sobs, and my eyes and nose grew hot and started to sting. It hurt when I breathed, and I was sopping wet with tears. After a while, the door opened a crack and I heard Mutsuki's voice. "I'm going," he said.

"I can't figure out what you're trying to say if you go on crying like that," Mizuho said over the phone. "What's wrong? Is Mutsuki there?"

"No," I said, hiccuping. "Mutsuki's—*hic*—at the hospital. He was—*hic*—on the night shift last night." I was still crying.

"And that's why you're crying like that?"

"Mutsuki was on the night shift...." I hiccuped again.

"Yeah, yeah, you said. And?"

"...Well, that's why."

"Shoko?"

I sobbed into the phone. I didn't even know why I was crying. "I drank whiskey in the bath. Mutsuki didn't call me. He always calls me when he's on the night shift. He bought donuts, but I said some things that were kind of mean. It wasn't even like I meant to, but——"

"Calm down," Mizuho said. "Did you call me up just to tell me how great Mutsuki is?"

"No——"

"Almost sounds like it. You're mad because usually he calls you and buys you donuts, and yesterday he didn't, right?"

"No," I wailed. "He *did* buy me donuts."

"Well, whatever." Mizuho sighed. "Why don't you guys just have a baby?"

"What are you talking about?"

"If you have a baby, everything will be fine. I used to get really lonely when my husband went away on business, but once I had Yuta, things got fine."

"But it's nothing like that."

"Yes, it is," Mizuho declared. "Think how worried your parents are going to be if you keep carrying on like this. And it's not fair to Mutsuki, either."

"But——"

"Why did you get married in the first place?"

I was silent for a while. "I dunno.... But I know it wasn't to have children," I answered weakly.

"Well, maybe not, but still…" she was saying as I hung up the phone. Mizuho didn't understand. There was no way she could understand. I was at a loss. "Think how worried your parents will be…. And it's not fair to Mutsuki, either."

"Well, it's certainly been a while," he said with a smile. He looked like an octopus, his broad forehead and reddish skin marked by a thousand wrinkles. His white doctor's coat was as worn-out looking as ever.

"You're looking well. What can I do for you today? Is there something you wanted to talk to me about?"

I didn't answer.

"I'm here to listen," he said, nodding encouragingly. He was the psychiatrist I had been seeing before I got married.

"How's married life been treating you?"

I told him it was going well.

"Good, I'm glad to hear it. It must be a big relief to your parents, too."

"But…" I said, but couldn't think of what to say next. Why was that such a relief to parents anyway?

"But?" he said.

"But I still get irritable, and depressed, and angry, like before. In fact, it's been getting worse lately, and—"

"And?" the doctor asked. I found his businesslike manner

amusing.

"And I've been really mean and cruel to my husband."

"For example?"

I explained. For example, there was what I'd said that very morning, the bitchy remarks of the day before, the mean jokes I'd played on him. But even as I went on, I knew I was wasting my time.

Doctor Octopus nodded seriously as I filled him in on the details of how I'd been behaving toward Mutsuki. "Really?" he said from time to time, or "Hmm, I see," or "Is that so?" or something else equally meaningless.

"And you've been behaving this way only with your husband, is that correct?"

I nodded.

"I see." He crossed his arms and sat in silence for a while, apparently deep in thought. But I knew it was just an act. He was only pretending to think. This was always what happened. I knew exactly what he was going to say next. Yet another one of his stock phrases. First his wrinkled face would break into a smile, and then he would start speaking earnestly and reassuringly, as if he had just come up with the perfect solution to the problem. You're fine. Nothing to worry about. It happens all the time.

"You're fine. Nothing to worry about. As far as I can tell, you're just feeling a little confused and upset as a result of all the adjustments you've had to make since you got married. It happens all the time." A big grin spread across his face as he spoke the last words.

I knew it. It was hopeless. He was contradicting himself again. After all, this was the same man who had told me that all I had to do was get married. Everything would be all right if I got married.

"Have you been having any trouble falling sleep?"

"No."

"What about your appetite?"

"It's okay."

"Good, good," said Doctor Octopus. "I don't need to give you anything for your nerves, then, or anything to help stimulate your appetite. Well, everything seems to be coming along just fine. I think the best advice I can give you now is to start thinking about starting a family. Everything will be fine once you have your first child."

Was this really the best he could come up with?

The trees along the road back to the station shone a beautiful dewy green, and there was a gentle breeze in the air. When it came down to it, I thought, all psychiatrists were the same. It's not as if this one was particularly bad. There was nothing anyone could do about it, and that was all there was to it. I bought a ticket at the window. Where *were* my "nerves," anyway? I'd never even seen them myself, so how was a doctor supposed to

be able to treat them? I looked up at the timetable and handed
in my ticket at the gate. There was a sharp crisp clip as the
ticket-collector punched my ticket. And then suddenly, something occurred to me. Or rather, some*one*: Dr. Kashibe. He was
a brain surgeon. He dealt with the brain, not just invisible
abstract things like "nerves."

It was a big hospital, and there were tropical plants growing
in the courtyard. I was led into a small, cramped room. The
white accordion shades that hung over all the windows made
me feel all the more claustrophobic.

"Doing a little hospital hopping, I see?" Dr. Kashibe said,
smiling. It was getting dark already, and in the courtyard outside
I could see groups of patients out for their evening walk. I nodded absent-mindedly as I watched the crows gathering in the
sky.

"You know, to tell you the truth," he said, "I hate chicken."

What? Startled, I looked at Dr. Kashibe. He had a pale com-
plexion, and finely drawn, clear-cut features. "Remember the
first time I came over to your apartment, and you served fried
chicken for dinner? I don't know how I managed to eat it."

"Oh." Had he heard any of what I had said?

"It was also strange for me to feel so comfortable, so much
at ease, with a woman I was meeting for the first time."

So comfortable, so much at ease? "Is this some kind of psychological treatment?" I asked.

"What do you mean by 'this'?"

"You know. They do it all the time. It's supposed to seem like we're just chatting, but really you're trying to delve into my innermost—"

Dr. Kashibe looked at me with a glint in his eyes and smiled. "Unfortunately, that kind of thing is beyond the range of a humble brain surgeon like me," he said. "No, I'm afraid I can't offer you any therapy," he said, opening a drawer, "but I can give you some medicine." He pulled out a black tin. It was a tin of hard candies.

"Here," he said, holding out his hand toward me. On his palm were five candies. Red. Green. Orange. Powdery. Round. I took them from him without a word.

A gust of wind blew in through the window, and the calendar on the wall fluttered slightly in the breeze.

Mizuho was waiting for me when I got home.

"Where've you been? I've been worried sick about you," she said. Mutsuki was already home. He was busy buttering crackers.

"I want you to tell me what's going on." Mizuho was angry. Yuta was asleep on the sofa.

"I was at the hospital. They gave me some really yummy medicine. Here, try some."

"What!" Mizuho shrieked. "I don't want any of your stupid medicine! What was that phone call all about anyway? You got me so worried!" She sounded crazy.

"Sorry," I said.

Mutsuki came over and joined me as I apologized, holding one hand up before him as if in prayer. "Sorry for all the trouble we've caused you," he said.

"Wait a minute! Why are you taking her side, Mutsuki?" Mizuho demanded. Her side! It sounded like the kind of thing an angry little kid would say. I couldn't help laughing out loud.

"It's not funny."

"Sorry," I said again. Mizuho went over to the refrigerator and took out a can of peach fizz, which she proceeded to down in one gulp.

"Are you trying to tell me I was freaking out about nothing? That's *so* not funny. And you, Mutsuki, won't you get a little mad, please?"

Mutsuki laughed as he opened a can of sardines. "I'm used to it," he said. Mizuho went on and on moaning and complaining, chomping on one after another of the sardine-topped crackers that Mutsuki kept handing to her. She'd finished three cans of peach fizz by the time she finally went home. She was still angry, though, and she kept on telling me how stupid she thought my behavior was, right up until the door shut behind her.

"Why don't we eat the donuts for dinner," I suggested.

Mutsuki said flat out that he'd rather not, but he went over and made some coffee right away. I laid out the silverware next to the plates. While we waited for the coffee to brew, I told Mutsuki about my visit to Dr. Kashibe. He looked shocked.

"What? You went to see Kashibe?"

I was surprised to see him so upset. "Yes. I thought it was a good idea, since he's a brain surgeon and all."

"It's totally different." I was taken aback by Mutsuki's tone. He had never been so curt with me before.

"Are you mad?"

No, he said, his voice already back to normal. "So what did he say?" he asked.

"He said it wasn't his field. Not his domain, or something."

Mutsuki coughed. "I'm a doctor, too, you know," he said.

"No." I looked down. I couldn't go to Mutsuki. It wouldn't do any good if I did. I'd just become more and more dependent on him, that's all.

Mutsuki broke the silence. "Hey, I'm pretty popular with patients, you know…" he said with a laugh. It made me sad to hear him making such a lame remark. It was so unlike him, so unnatural.

"Just because you're good doesn't mean you're the right doctor for me." I was surprised at the edginess of my own words. I stuffed a donut into my mouth to prevent myself from uttering anything more.

"So I guess the in-house doctor is disqualified, then," Mutsuki said, pouring the coffee. Silently, I put the rest of the donut in my mouth. The coffee was weak but hot, and the raisins were soft and sweet. I could taste the oil and sugar mixing in my mouth, and I felt like crying again.

MIDDAY MOON

· ·

Shoko's been acting really depressed lately. She spends most of her time brooding, staring off into space in sullen silence. Just when I'm least expecting it, she'll blurt out something really aggressive and confrontational. Next thing I know, her eyes are welling up with tears again for no obvious reason, and she's looking over at me with this horrible pathetic look in her eyes. Everyone has their ups and downs, I guess, but Shoko's are a little extreme. I've learned that it's best not to get too upset or to show too much concern, and anyway, I like Shoko best when she's herself. But even so, I've started to wonder recently if it was really such a good idea to let things go on like this for so long. Her attempts to improve the situation by going to see her old doctor and dropping in on Kashibe made my heart ache. Always fighting her battles alone.

"What's on your mind?" Kon asked. I was lying on his small and uncomfortable bed, with its beat-up old mattress and striped sheets. Kon's bed.

"Lemme guess, actually." Kon was hunched over on the floor, clipping his toenails. "Your mom, right? You said at dinner she came by at the hospital."

"Wrong."

Next to the pillow, Kon's clock was flashing 1 a.m. It had a huge digital display, and an alarm that went right through you when it went off. Next to the clock was a lamp and a potted cactus.

"Did you have to remind me of that?" I said. "No, I was thinking about Shoko. I'm worried about her. She's getting more and more unstable every day."

"I'm not surprised," Kon said, as unconcerned as ever as he rolled up the tissue he'd been using to catch his toenails in. "I mean, it figures with her husband cheating on her like this. Who wouldn't?" I looked down at Kon's straight bare back, and tossed him his T-shirt, which had been lying crumpled on a pile on top of the bed. Kon knew all too well the effect his slim tanned body had on me.

"Put that on. You'll catch cold."

He stood up straight, bathed in the moonlight that came streaking in through the blinds, his shadow stretched in stripes across the floor in front of him.

"Well I'm sorry, but I like being naked."

As I showered, I remembered the way Mother had looked when she'd stopped by the hospital that afternoon: so serious. "I hear the success rates are very high," she'd said. "Why the hesitance? If you won't explain your reasons to us, how can you expect us to understand?" She'd gone on and on about artificial insemination: how safe it was, the wonderful success rates lately. And then she'd given me a long passionate speech about the vital role of children in a family, and about all the joys they brought into your life.

"I'm sure her parents are hoping you'll have a child soon, too." Mother paused and heaved a dramatic sigh. She was staring down at the ashtray on the table. "When I think of all the happiness you're depriving Shoko of, it makes me so very unhappy. It could mean divorce, you know, if they ever found out."

"Oh, Mother." I sat down across from her and looked her straight in the face. Her lusterless skin, her carefully plucked eyebrows, her thin painted lips, the small beauty mark just below her right eye.

"We're just not ready," I said. "Shoko and I don't feel right about having children yet."

A strange look of satisfaction overtook Mother's face. "But that's what we're here for," she said, smiling gently. "We'll do everything we can to help. It's all right, you know. Everyone's nervous at first." I caught a whiff of the perfume she always wore, and felt my stomach turn.

When I came back from the bathroom, Kon was whirring the juicer. His health potion of choice was fresh vegetable juice mixed with egg yolk.

"So what did you think of the lubricant?" he said. Kon had bought a new mint-and-lime-scented lubricant for us to use when we made love. In the past, we'd always stuck to creams that were fragrance-free, and at first, I objected that I didn't want to use anything scented (and especially not something like mint, which I thought would seep into my skin). "Says here that it's all natural ingredients, though," Kon had said. "Easy on the skin." And so eventually I'd agreed to give it a try.

"It was okay, huh?"

I grunted agreement and took a bottle of Evian from the refrigerator. Shoko was over at her parents' place. In fact, she was the one who had suggested that I come over and stay with Kon, since it had been so long. "I'll probably end up having to stay the night," she had argued. "I'm sure my parents will be happy to have me. I *am* their only daughter, after all."

"*Now* what's on your mind?" Kon asked me.

"Nothing," I said, but he didn't fall for that. He laughed and gave me one of his "Oh yeah?" looks.

"Hey Mutsuki, why don't you just sleep with Shoko?" He said it casually enough, but something in his voice told me he was quite serious. I was so taken aback that I didn't know what to say. Then I started to feel really annoyed. How could he say such things?

"Do you mind not kidding me about stuff like that?" I

requested.

"You don't feel sorry for her?" he asked. "I wouldn't mind. I mean, I'm not one of those dime-novel queers, remember, who find all women repulsive." He poured the thick green brew he had just concocted into a cup, and looked over at me solemnly. "You've never even tried it, have you?"

I told him to cut it out. I gulped down my Evian, which seemed to have no taste at all that night. "You got anything stronger?" I asked.

"Booze? I think there's still half a bottle of gin lying around somewhere." He asked me if I wanted to watch a film, picking out a tape. Some B-grade American action flick. "Cool car chases."

Gin, huh? Too bad there's no kummel, I thought. I was surprised to find myself thinking such a thing. I'd never even heard of it until fairly recently.

And so we settled down in front of the TV and watched Kon's lousy movie screech its way to its ear-splitting climax while he worked on his vegetable sludge and I sipped my gin on the rocks. It was yet another of the pointless blood-splattered movies Kon seemed to enjoy so much.

It was four by the time I left Kon's. The roads were deserted. Great, I thought, I should be able to get home by five, have a nice long soak in the bath, and eat a proper breakfast.

After all, I wanted to start the day out right, even if it was a Saturday and there was nothing I really needed to do.

Outside, pale early morning light washed across the sky, the moon and the stars now little more than dimming lights fixed in the fast-fading darkness. Street lamps shone on indecisively. Driving home at dawn like this reminded me of my student days, when I used to spend every night at Kon's place, leaving while the rest of the world was still asleep. One after another, the familiar old sights were coming back: the moon in the brightening sky, faint and pale over the highway fences; the green emergency phones every few miles; the exit signs. Driving like that, I felt as if I had gone back in time.

I took off my shoes at the door and stepped into the apartment. I turned into the living room. And there on my left, by the doorway, was Shoko flopped down on the floor.

"Whoa!" I shouted in surprise, but there was no reaction. I could see that she'd been crying. There wasn't a single light on.

"I'm home."

"Welcome back," said Shoko. Her face was expressionless. There was no sign of movement. She was staring fixedly at the Cézanne on the wall.

"You didn't go over to your mother's?"

"I did, but I came back."

Gosh, she looked depressed. Haunted. The air felt heavy and stagnant all around her.

"You been sitting there all night?"

"I was singing for the purple man. Then he said he'd sing something back to me, so I've been sitting here waiting and waiting, but he won't sing at all."

I was still in a state of shock. I could feel blood retreat from my fingertips. "Shoko?"

Shoko sat still, staring unblinkingly ahead at the painting on the wall. What should I do now, I wondered. Put her to bed? Try and talk things over with her? Maybe she'd start to feel better after a bath, or a glass of warm milk?

"I'm kidding," Shoko said with a straight face. "He's just a painting. He can't sing." She got up and went out on the veranda. She probably just wanted to get away from me. I was always making such a big deal about everything.

"You can still see the stars." She got out the telescope and peered into it. So pale and faint, she said. "You can't count on anything, can you? Not even the moon and the stars."

What the hell was going on? Baffled, I went and changed out of my suit. Then I washed my hands and made some coffee. Shoko was still peering into the telescope. I dusted off my shoes and put them away on the shoe rack, and brushed the lint off my suit and put it back in the closet. I poured the coffee into our morning mugs and looked over to the veranda. Shoko was still standing in the same position, hunched over the telescope.

"Shoko!" I shouted over to her. No response. Amazing the

way she could stay in that position for so long without her back hurting. I went to get myself a chair. It was still early morning, and it was cold out on the veranda. It didn't feel much like spring.

One eye still glued to the telescope, Shoko stood dripping silent tears—not a sob, not a sniff, not a hiccup. There was a strange tenseness in the air.

"Shoko?"

I put my arms around her from behind and tried to drag her away from the telescope, but it was useless. She tensed up and hugged the telescope like a child. She was sobbing now. "Leave me alone, I'm fine," she said in a weak crushed voice between sobs. And then, suddenly, the floodgates opened, she started bawling, and the tears came in torrents. She had given herself up entirely to her crying, with no energy left to resist. I dragged her back into the apartment. I spoke to her in a soft voice, trying to coax some kind of response out of her. "What's wrong?" I asked. "Please stop crying." No reaction.

I took a sip of coffee. Calm down, calm down.

"Why won't you tell me what's wrong?" I said.

Shoko stiffened again, and stopped crying. She raised her tear-stained face and glared at me. "Don't use your doctor's voice on me." There was hostility in her eyes. "I'm not one of your patients, you know."

Shoko grabbed my cup of coffee and drank it down in one

gulp. "Just now," she began, wiping her mouth angrily with the back of her hand. She was seething, boiling over with a rage she didn't know how to express. "You thought I'd really gone crazy, didn't you? Like, I guess she really does have problems, waiting all night for the purple man to sing? She's really flipped this time, that's what you were thinking I bet.

"But that's not how it is at all," she said, and started to cry again. "You just don't get it, Mutsuki. It's not like that at all," she kept insisting, hiccuping and sniffling in between sobs. She was so upset she couldn't even string a sentence together. This was shaping up into a real tragedy.

"I understand, I understand, it's okay," I said, crouching down next to her, waiting for her to stop crying. "I'm going to heat up the bath. Why don't you warm up a bit first and then we'll have some breakfast."

I got breakfast ready while Shoko soaked in the bath. At first I thought I'd make her pancakes, her favorite, but I didn't want to be accused of treating her like an invalid in need of spoiling. I decided to make some cheese-on-toast and salad instead. I got a bottle of low-alcohol champagne (less than 2%, suitable for children) and stuck it in the freezer to chill. I'd often seen champagne on breakfast menus in hotels overseas, and one time I'd tried it out at home. Shoko had loved it, and since then it had become one of our little treats: champagne with breakfast.

Shoko was in the bath for two whole hours. She always liked

to take her time in the bath, but the exact length of time she
spent there was inversely proportional to how happy she was
feeling. The worse her mood, the longer her bathing. By the
time she came out, though, she seemed much more relaxed.
She was wearing a white T-shirt and faded jeans. She toweled off
her hair and plopped herself down on the sofa. I used the champagne stirrer to conjure up some bubbles, and handed her a
glass of the clear golden liquid. She sipped at it quietly.

"Hmm, that's good, thanks," she noted in a voice empty of
emotion.

"How was your mom?" I was only making conversation, but
it was enough to make Shoko frown and put up her guard again.

"Fine."

"Was your dad there too?"

She was glaring at me now, a look of protest in her eyes. "My
parents are both fine. Nanako and Fava Bean were there too, and
they were both fine, too." She was making it quite clear that she
didn't want to discuss the matter any further.

"I see," I said gently, backing off. Nanako and Fava Bean were
her father's beloved Java sparrows.

"Your mother called last night," Shoko said casually, lifting
up a piece of cheese-on-toast and studying it closely. "Just wondering how we were doing, that's all."

Mother? Now it was my turn to tense up. But that was all
Shoko had to say on the subject. She washed down her toast

with the champagne.

"Tell me a story about Kon," she said. "Tell me about when you fight."

"God, I don't know. We've had so many," I said.

Tell me about the worst one then, she said.

Our worst fight ever?

"It was back when Kon was still in middle school," I said. "There was this girl who had a big crush on him, and one day she came to ask me to help her out. Kon and I were next door neighbors in those days, really close. I felt sorry for her, so I set them up on a date. I begged Kon to go along with it. Just that once, you know, as a favor to me. But you know Kon. 'No way,' he said, 'I don't wanna go, so I'm not gonna go.' You can imagine. So I said fine, what if I come along too? And so finally, I got him to agree, but just barely. As if I would really tag along on someone else's date. I showed up with an excuse that I'd made up. Something had come up and I couldn't be their chaperone. Kon totally freaked out. He squatted down right in the middle of the crosswalk, refusing to budge until I promised to come with them. All around us, cars are honking away like crazy. The poor girl who had the crush on Kon is absolutely livid. You can imagine. Kon can be impossible to deal with sometimes. So there he is, sitting in the middle of the road, shouting his head off: 'You're the worst. You can't even keep a promise! It's not human!' So I'm like fine, whatever, come on let's get off the road, it's not safe sitting here like that. We finally cross the street and I tell him, 'Well, see you tomorrow.' At this he lets out a big roar like a bear and comes right at me. I was stunned. He was only a kid, but he was really violent and I couldn't do anything to hold him back. In the end, it turned into a real fight; I mean, we were really laying into each other. We even got taken into custody and everything. Now that I think about it, though, it was that poor girl who came out of it the worst. She was crying the whole time at the police station."

"Poor thing. Getting your heart broken really sucks," Shoko said with unexpected feeling. "Was that after you guys were already together?"

"Just before."

"Oh," she said, looking off into the distance, as if lost in her own memories. "You go way back, you and Kon."

I didn't know what to say to that, so I just nibbled at my toast.

"I really like Kon, you know," she said suddenly, and poured herself some more of the fake champagne. She waited for me to stir it up and then sipped at it slowly. "Too bad Kon can't have your baby, huh?"

That floored me. I was speechless for a while. I knew all of a sudden what Mother's phone call had been about.

"Don't worry about whatever Mother said."

Her expression grew tense.

"Mizuho was telling me to have a baby, too, the last time we talked. It's only natural, she said. *And* Doctor Octopus. But he said the same thing about getting married, too. Everyone's so weird. Why do they all have to tell me to have a baby?" Contrary to my expectations, though, Shoko didn't start crying. "I just wish we could stay like this."

"We can," I said.

"My mom said I was being selfish when I went to see her. That I wasn't being fair to you. Or them."

"That's not true," I said, but Shoko wasn't listening.

"We had a big fight. I decided not to stay over and came back home. But then your mother called, around nine. And she said why don't we talk to Dr. Kakii about artificial insemination, and stuff." Shoko looked upset and confused. "What's wrong with them?" she asked. "Why can't things just stay the way they are? We're so natural like this."

Whatever exactly she meant by "natural", the confidence with which she made the assertion made me feel warm and fuzzy.

Shoko piled up the breakfast dishes. "I'm just gonna take a quick nap," she said, and stood up. "You want to sleep too? I'll iron the sheets for you."

"Yeah, good idea. Let's both have a nap." I carried the dishes over to the sink. "Don't bother about ironing the sheets, though. It's gotten warmer."

It was a winter thing, to iron out the sheets. I didn't hear any reply, so I turned off the faucet and shouted, "You don't have to iron the bed, okay?" But I didn't hear any response. When I turned around, Shoko was still standing in the corner of the kitchen.

"What, you been there the whole time?"

"You said it was my job to iron the bed," Shoko said. She looked desperate. "If the sheets feel too hot, you could wait until they cool down. I thought you said you liked it when the sheets are all sharp and clean."

"...Yes, you're right," I said. I had no choice but to agree, she looked so frantic. Her face, which looked so determined just moments ago, was now helplessly scrunched up. Pale, small, feeble. As I watched her go into the bedroom to do the ironing, I knew that I was the one making her feel so cornered. It was breaking my heart.

CAGE OF WATER

. .

It was years since the last time I'd been to an amusement park. I was standing next to the ticket booth by the entrance waiting for Mizuho, watching the families, couples, and noisy schoolgirls. Mutsuki was supposed to have come too, but someone had paged him early that morning and he'd dropped everything to run off to work.

Mutsuki was in internal medicine, so he hardly ever got paged. In most emergencies—road accidents, acute appendicitis—it was usually the surgeons who were needed. Most of the time when Mutsuki's pager rang, it meant that a patient's condition had deteriorated. And since Mutsuki spent most of his time in the geriatric ward, this normally meant that someone had died. Mutsuki was like a zombie for days whenever one of his patients died. He lost his appetite, too. He felt bad about it, as if it were his fault. He used to go on about how ashamed he felt that he hadn't been able to do anything for the deceased. Professional responsibility and all that. My reaction was exactly the opposite. I blamed the patient. Making a decent, kind-hearted person like Mutsuki feel so terrible about himself. It was probably wrong of me to think that way, but I couldn't help it. I felt like summoning the person over, whoever it was (well, the soul, anyway) for a few *serious words* behind the school gym. If you're gonna die, that's your own business. Just don't go dragging Mutsuki into it!

Anyway, as soon as I realized Mutsuki wasn't going to be able to make it, the whole amusement park idea started to lose its appeal. I wanted to cancel too, but Mutsuki begged me not to. It wouldn't be fair to Mizuho, he said. And so in the end I had agreed to turn up, and now here I was waiting for her. Maybe the day out would do me good, I figured. Maybe it would help me forget unpleasant things for a short while. My mother was driving me nuts recently. Mutsuki's mother, too, for that matter. But now I was already starting to regret it. What was I doing there anyway, standing next to the stupid ticket booth? On the other side of the fence, the amusement park seemed to stretch on forever, a huge expanse of colorful steel. The cheerful music blaring out of the speakers everywhere just made things worse. It was so forced, so unnatural.

"Shoko-chan!" Someone was calling me. A voice from about a million years ago. I turned around to find Haneki standing there waving at me.

"It's been a long time." He was wearing jeans and a polo shirt, a striped jacket thrown over his tall, lanky frame.

Next to him was Mizuho. She looked uncomfortable, as if she didn't know what to say. "We just happened to bump into each other...I thought it might be nice if we all...."

Yeah right. As if anyone just randomly decides to go to an amusement park all alone.

"How are you!" Yuta exclaimed. For some reason the brat's hellos were always really formal. A formulaic politeness oblivious to the ambience of the moment. No sense of timing.

"How are you!" he said again, loud. He was obviously not going to give up until I gave some kind of response. His innocent self-confidence got on my nerves. When I returned his greeting, he grabbed on to my right hand and gripped hold of my fingers.

"You haven't changed," Haneki said quietly, averting his eyes and looking down at the ground for no apparent reason. He was always doing that. His hair was blown back in the breeze, exposing his forehead, as care-worn and worried-looking as ever. Strange to think that I had once been so in love with that wrinkled old forehead of his.

"I still get that feeling, you know, like your body is here but your soul is off on a trip someplace else."

"You haven't changed either," I said. I felt like telling him I didn't have a clue what he was trying to say, but I held my tongue. I threw Mizuho a look as if to say, What the hell were you thinking?

"I hear you're married now."

I looked down at Haneki's shoes. I had to smile. He hadn't changed a bit. Black leather ankle boots. He used to wear them all the time. I had told him a million times what I thought of them, but he never paid any attention to what I said. It was already summer, a hot Sunday afternoon at the amusement park, but he was wearing them anyway. His feet must have been going through hell.

"And what about *Mr.* Minamizawa?" I said, turning towards Mizuho. What was it with everyone's husbands today?

"Decided to stay at home. Said he was too exhausted to move. You know what they're like, those poor overworked salarymen."

"Hmm."

We bought our tickets and went into the park. Mizuho didn't ask about Mutsuki.

Amusement parks are strange places. Even if you don't feel like going at first, you often wind up enjoying it in spite of yourself. You don't really have any choice in the matter. It's not like it's particularly fun or anything, but there's something about an amusement park that pretty much *forces* you to play along. It demands 100% of your energy and concentration. We fell in line, and conquered the rides one by one. Surprisingly enough, Haneki and Yuta seemed to get along really well, and the two of them went running happily together from one ride to the next.

"I always used to think of him as this decadent young the-atrical type, but he's actually pretty cheerful," Mizuho said. Decadent? Where did she get that one from? I was taken aback, and I looked her straight in the face.

"He *is* cheerful," I said, in a voice so forceful and insistent it came out sounding almost resentful. As if I were really saying, How come you never realized it until now? This time it was Mizuho's turn to look surprised.

She was wearing sunglasses and orange lipstick, and had more make-up on than usual. Her beige hat was pulled low over her eyes, as if to show the world that she at least wasn't taking any chances with the evil UV rays.

"Hey, look!" Haneki and Yuta had found someone dressed up like a big, furry animal, and they were jumping up and down, shouting and waving at us. I hate those stupid mascot charac-ters, but I guess they're pretty much inevitable in an amusement park. The wobbly out-of-proportion three-part bodies, the arti-ficial smiles, the weird way of walking—it was just plain creepy to me. I knew Mizuho felt the same way, but that didn't stop her from fishing a camera out of her straw shoulder bag and running over to them, waving frantically.

We sat at a table underneath a big umbrella and had pizza and soda for lunch. Believe it or not, there wasn't a single can of beer to be had in the whole park. As if spending the day with a child in tow wasn't enough of an achievement for me.

"Okay, a joke's a joke. Don't you think it's about time someone told me what's really going on here?" I said, stabbing with a
toothpick at the olives I'd been saving over from the pizza.
Neither of them said a word. I figured my best strategy was to
try Mizuho first. "You knew Mutsuki wasn't coming, didn't
you?" I said, trying to sound as light-hearted and so-what about
it as possible. "And you asked Haneki to come instead."

Mizuho had this really serious look on her face. "Yes, you're
right," she said. She had taken off her hat and sunglasses.
Sunlight shone back at me from the rim of the table.

"Why?"

"Why? Where's the harm in it anyway?" Haneki spoke up. "I
mean, it's been so long, and aren't we having a good time?" He
looked over at Yuta for support, but Yuta seemed not to notice
him. He had pizza sauce all over his face.

It didn't make any sense. What could Mizuho have been
thinking? I couldn't work it out at all.

"Who's up for a ride on the log flume?" Haneki asked. We'd
been avoiding it so far, since Yuta couldn't go on anything too
fast, but the truth was that it was my favorite ride. Haneki must
have known this—he was deliberately prodding me where I was
softest. I hated it that he knew me so well. I didn't say anything.

"You guys go ahead," Mizuho said.

Haneki got up and smiled at Yuta. "Why don't you get your
mom to buy you some ice cream or something?"

The log flume wasn't very far away. In fact, it was practically next door to the pizza house. Well, what do you know, I thought. He'd only suggested it because we happened to be so close. For some reason, that made me feel much happier about everything.

"Funny, out with another man's wife like this," Haneki said, sitting down and fastening his seat belt. I had to admit, it did feel pretty weird. I buckled up next to him. At that angle, he looked just like the Haneki I used to know, back in the days when he used to take me out on drives. The same pale thin lips, the same scraggly hair. Why doesn't he just get it cut, I always used to think. A stressed attendant rushed past, checking everyone's seat belts.

"What's he like, your husband?"

"Oh, he's really nice."

As soon as I'd spoken the words, I started to feel really depressed. It felt wrong, talking about Mutsuki so casually. As if I could sum him up with a trite phrase. "Oh, he's really nice." No, Mutsuki was much more...much more what? I was confused. I couldn't find the words for it. How was I supposed to explain Mutsuki to someone who wanted to know what he was like?

"I haven't seen that look for a while, Wrinkle-brows," he commented.

There was a loud noise as the buzzer sounded, and we

moved off with a jolt. I grabbed on to the handle bar.

"Hey, we're not doing anything wrong, so stop looking like that, okay? Like I always used to say, your wildness is one of the things I like best about you."

I was as clueless as ever about what he meant by that. But the log flume was wonderful. The excitement and anticipation as we climbed slowly higher and higher; the speed of the drop; the thrill of the sharp sudden turns, of being rattled about inside the car like the contents of a lunch box; the splashing jets of water. I loved every second of it. Sunlight glinted off the silver handle bar and dazzled my eyes. I looked down, and saw Haneki's huge black boots. They obviously hadn't been polished in a while, and they were filthy with dust. For Mutsuki, that would have been unthinkable.

The cars slid to a halt when we got back to the start of the ride, and there was a vague buzz of excitement as people unfastened their seat belts and climbed up out of the cars.

Haneki leaned over towards me and said something, his words almost swallowed up in the commotion around us. "Can't we still get together like this once in a while? As *good friends*?" He used the English expression.

Good friends? What was I supposed to say to that? We stepped out of the car and back onto solid ground. I still felt a little wobbly.

"You shouldn't blame Mizuho-chan, you know. She was only

doing what your husband asked," Haneki added as we walked down the stairs. I felt every hair on my body stand up on end.

"Did you just say 'your' husband?"

Mizuho and Yuta were waiting for us at the exit.

"Hey! Whose husband asked who to do what?"

"Mutsuki asked me...to invite Haneki-san along," Mizuho said. My head was spinning.

While Haneki and Yuta were off being whizzed around on the tea cup ride, Mizuho told me about the phone call she'd had the day before. Mutsuki's stupid phone call. Apparently Mutsuki had already decided he wasn't going to come with us.

"I tried to find out why, but he wouldn't tell me. And then he said he had a favor he wanted to ask me. 'I know this is going to sound strange,' he said, 'but do you know Haneki, Shoko's old boyfriend?'" Mizuho was talking really fast. She sounded angry. "I said, 'Of course I know him. We used to double-date and stuff.' Then he asked me if I could invite Haneki to come along instead. I didn't know what to say. I asked him why, and he said, 'Well, Shoko's been kind of depressed these days. Unstable.' I said, 'Yeah, and so?' Then Mutsuki got all serious and told me, 'I think it would be a good idea if she had a boyfriend'! I mean, can you believe it? I disagreed, of course. But he just laughed and said, 'I'm no good for her like that, you see. I'm not exactly cut out for the part.' And then all serious again, 'But it's not like just any old guy will do.'"

My blood was seething with rage. I felt like going home right then and beating the crap out of him. How could he? My eyes started to fill with tears. I shut them tight, but teardrops squeezed through my eyelids and ran down my cheeks, burning hot. I won't forgive him, I thought. I'll never forgive him for this.

I started to walk away, but Mizuho grabbed hold of my wrist.

"Now it's your turn to explain," she said. "What's going on? Are things not going well between you guys?"

Now the tears were really starting to flow. My throat felt hot, and I started to sob. I must have looked like a monkey or something, with my face all red. People kept looking over at us, but I didn't care. So even the call on his pager this morning had been part of the plan. And I'd been so worried about him, hoping he wasn't going to get depressed or start losing his appetite again. I had even been angry at the dead. I snatched Mizuho's bag, which just happened to be close to hand, and started scattering its contents on the ground. Her yellow hand towel, her make-up case, her address book, her brown leather sunglass case, her hairbrush, Yuta's cookies. And what about Haneki? God, what an idiot! Did he have no shame? Playing along with their stupid schemes, doing just anything they asked him to do. I crouched down and wept like a child.

Mizuho got down next to me and patted me on the shoulder, but I couldn't stop crying. Yuta and Haneki came back from the ride, and a small group of people gathered around us. I could hear voices. "Is she having a seizure?" someone said.

In the end, I was put on a stretcher for the first time in my life and carried into the infirmary. They lifted me onto a hard white bed. I didn't care what happened to me anymore. I didn't even have the energy to cry. An old woman in a white uniform pried my eyes open with her fingers and examined my pupils. "You still alive in there?" she asked. She took off my shoes and pressed a cold towel to my head. "You just take it easy for a while and then we'll see how you feel," she said, as she took hold of my wrist. "Oh dear, your pulse is racing."

I felt like telling her she was wasting her time, but it did feel nice to have the cold towel over my eyes and a breeze blowing over my stockinged feet. There must have been a window open somewhere. Happy music and cheerful voices. I remembered how once a long time ago I had skipped gym class and spent an hour stretched out like this in the infirmary at school.

"I'm definitely going to call Mutsuki," Mizuho said anxiously. "Wherever he is, I'm sure they'll be able to contact him."

"I don't think that's such a good idea. Shoko-chan's a passionate woman. I mean, she's just wildly impulsive sometimes. She'll probably calm down again in half an hour or so. I don't think you need to bother her husband."

"That's not the point," Mizuho snapped. "What I mean is,

this is his fault."

I could feel someone's breath against my cheek. I opened my eyes slightly to take a look. From under the towel on my eyes, I could make out Yuta's T-shirt. He was leaning against the bed, peering down at me. I must have been quite a sight. I felt his eyes boring into the left side of my face. He wouldn't turn away. It was starting to freak me out. I didn't know what to do. Eventually I couldn't take it any more, and I poked my hand out from under the sheets. He hesitated for a moment, and then he reached out a trembling little hand and rested it on top of mine.

A tiny, warm, moist little hand.

By the time Mutsuki came in, I had drifted off into a light sleep. From the furthest reaches of my consciousness I could hear their voices: Mutsuki thanking the nurse, Mizuho nagging Mutsuki, Mutsuki and Haneki going through the motions of a formal introduction. Mutsuki came over towards the bed, slowly. I strained my senses, trying to feel him with my whole body. His footsteps. His presence.

He moved the towel aside and brushed away the hairs that had stuck to my forehead. His dry palm was warm like autumn sunlight.

"I'm sorry."

He touched a finger to my eyelids and spoke in a voice so low I couldn't catch what he was saying. He knows I'm awake, I thought. It's like being in a cage of water. Gentle entrapment. Mutsuki understood exactly what I was going through, just as I knew everything about him. About Haneki, about the fake call on his pager. I couldn't feel angry at him anymore. I felt Mutsuki's finger against my eyelid. Why did we always have to torture each other?

"Shoko. Shoko." Mizuho shook my leg, trying to wake me.

"It's all right. I'll take her home like this. I came in the car," Mutsuki said, and I shivered. I was almost scared. I can say for sure that I couldn't have gone home that day except by pretending to be asleep. That's a certainty.

Mutsuki slid his arms underneath me, and as he lifted me up I buried my face in his chest. I could feel his warmth, his heartbeat. I felt comforted, like a child. Even though we had never made love, his body seemed to fit mine naturally.

Out in the parking lot, endless lines of cars glinted in the light of the setting sun. My body rocking to the rhythm of Mutsuki's gait, I squinted through half-opened eyes for his beat-up old jalopy. Small and dark blue, Mutsuki's beloved car.

"I guess we'll take the train back then," Haneki said.

As they walked away, Mizuho got in her parting shot. "I look forward to finding out what this is all about tomorrow," she said.

I felt bad that I hadn't said thank you to the old lady in the white uniform.

"Take care," I heard her say as we left the infirmary. The only thing I could remember about her was her legs: long thin swishing legs, like sticks.

Even after we made it to the car, I kept on pretending to be asleep. Mutsuki didn't say anything, he just put on one of my favorite cassettes. As we wound our way slowly along the coastal road, I started to think of home. The veranda with its white railing, the purple man, Kon's tree. I wanted to hurry up and get back as soon as possible. With my eyes still closed, I opened the window. The sweet strains of Julie's singing wafted softly into the evening sky.

SILVER LIONS

• •

When I got back from the hospital, Shoko was in the living room watching TV. Pretty intently, by the look of things. "Hi, I'm home," I said, but her eyes were glued to the 25-inch screen.

She mumbled, "Welcome back."

We'd bought the TV on an installment plan. Right now, I could see vast dusty plains rolling across the screen.

"What are you watching?"

"Television," was Shoko's instant reply. Apparently she wasn't being deliberately obnoxious, so I just shrugged my shoulders and decided to take her answer at face value. I changed out of my work clothes and cleaned my shoes, then went into the bathroom to freshen up. By the time I got back to the living room, the program was over.

"What would you like for dinner?" I called out, rummaging through the refrigerator. Anything, she answered distractedly, as if her mind was still lost somewhere inside the TV set. There was still some meat left over from the hamburgers we'd had the day before, so I decided to use it to make some meatballs. Egg and meatball soup.

"So what was the program about?" I asked, choosing my words more carefully this time.

"It was a documentary. On wildlife," Shoko explained. "There was this gazelle that had some disease and it kept going round in circles until it dropped dead. And then they showed this baby elephant that tripped over its own trunk and fell down. Zebras mating, a pack of hyenas eating a gnu." I could hear the excitement in her voice as she went on. "Apparently a gnu can smell rain from 50 kilometers away. But they're weak. And they have so many enemies. Lions and hyenas and cheetahs. Lots of animals kill gnus every day."

Shoko told me all about the gnus while I got dinner ready. She wasn't skimping on any details now. I was treated to a particularly graphic description of how the gnus had been killed and eaten. How quickly the hyenas tore apart their prey, how greedy the vultures were. They even picked out the meat from between the ribs, she reported.

"Even the baby lions!" she said. "Their little noses were all covered in blood. They stick their whole head in and just gobble it up."

I looked from the neat line of freshly prepared meatballs to Shoko's face, and said nothing.

During dinner, Shoko still seemed distracted. (In the end, the meal was a simple one of egg soup and sauteed mushrooms.) The images had obviously had a big impact on her.

"You want to go out somewhere tomorrow?" I said, in an attempt to haul her back to reality. "How about a movie? It's been so long since we did anything like that."

Shoko said she'd promised to go see Mizuho. It was already a week since that day at the amusement park, and she still owed Mizuho an explanation.

"Do you want me to come with you?"

Shoko shook her head. "I won't be long. Besides, it's Sunday. Your big clean-up day."

Clean-up! Ah, how appealing that concept was. All that dust piled up behind the shoe closet, the mold in between the tiles in the bathroom.... I was like a man primed for battle.

After dinner, Shoko made tea for three. One cup for me, one for herself, and one for the *yucca elephantipes*.

"Have you ever heard of the silver lions?" Shoko said as she poured rum into the tea.

"Is this another of your blood-and-guts nature stories?" I asked.

"No," Shoko frowned. "No, it's a legend."

"Oh, a legend?" That was a relief. I took a sip of the rum tea. "Tell me about it," I said. "What's the story?"

The legend according to Shoko went like this: once every

generation, large numbers of white lions are born in different places around the world, all at the same time. Their coats are so light in color that the other lions refuse to accept them, and before long they disappear from the pride.

Shoko went on:

"But really they're magic lions, you see. They leave the pride and go off to live in a group by themselves. They don't eat meat; they're herbivorous. And then, nobody really knows for sure why, but they all die young. They're not very strong to begin with, and they never really eat very much, so they die off really easily. From the heat or the cold, even. They live up in the rocks, and when you see their manes blow in the wind they look more silver than white. It's supposed to be really beautiful."

Shoko was telling me all this without any obvious emotion. Herbivorous lions that die from the heat? I'd never heard anything like it. I didn't know what I was supposed to say. Shoko looked me in the face and said, "Sometimes you guys kind of remind me of the silver lions."

I was confused. "You guys"? Meaning me and Kon and Kakii and Kashibe? I didn't know what to say. Shoko downed what was left of her rum tea, presumably stone cold by now, and then poured the other cup into the plant's pot.

"Kon's tree likes its tea with one cube of sugar and half a teaspoonful of rum," she said.

The next morning Shoko left the house at around ten and I got straight to work on the cleaning, a Bach CD playing in the background. I scrubbed the bathroom, polished the pans, and dusted the apartment from top to bottom. I vacuumed the floor, and then rinsed everything down with a mop. I was just wondering whether to clean the windows too when the phone rang. It was my father. He said he was calling from the station.

"Mind if I stop by? I won't stay long. No, that's okay, I already ate. What, you haven't had lunch yet? It's 2:30 already."

"Is Mother with you?"

"No, just me. Is Shoko home?"

"She's out. If you'd told us you were coming, we'd have made sure we were both here."

"Oh, it's not worth making a fuss over a visit from me," he said, and laughed awkwardly.

Shoko got back as soon as I hung up. "Present for you," she said, holding out a plastic bag. Inside was a goldfish. Apparently there had been some kind of bonsai sale near Mizuho's place, and there'd been a stall set up selling goldfish.

"Wow, this takes me back."

Shoko seemed to be big on living things these days. She took a packet of fish food from her skirt pocket and put it down on the table.

"My father called to say he's coming over," I said as I transferred the goldfish into a bowl.

"When?" Shoko asked, surprised. I looked at my watch. Another five or six minutes, I told her. Back in a sec, she said, heading back toward the front door. She put her shoes back on and opened the door again.

"Where're you going?"

"To get something to have with the tea."

"Oh, don't worry," I said.

Shoko shook her head. "Mizuho told me I should. When people come over, you have to have something to give them. That's the kind of thing that would *never* occur to me. Like when your parents came over before, all we had was tea and things that *I* like, like cucumbers and tomatoes and cheese."

"That's all right. Don't worry about it."

"And that's not all," Shoko said firmly. "Mizuho was really preachy today. She said I should listen hard like it was her last will and testament. I'm truly honored to have had such a person as my friend."

I was confused. "You're talking about her as if she's really dead."

"Oh no," Shoko said, laughing. "As if any dead person could go on the way she does. She told me I need to be more considerate. To be a good wife. It's not like I don't *know* what I'm supposed to do, I just need to be more considerate. Well, that's what Mizuho says anyway."

I was silent.

"Oh God, your father will be here any minute," she said, and with that rushed out of the apartment.

He arrived as soon as she left. It was turning into a pretty hectic Sunday.

"Did you see Shoko on your way in?"

No. His short hair was about seven-tenths gray.

"Hmm, maybe she went the other way. She was here for a minute just now, but then she had to go out again. I told her you were coming, so I don't think she'll be long," I said, pouring some coffee.

"Sounds like an excuse to me," he said. Suddenly I felt awkward, without really knowing why. I had a bad feeling. He continued, "Actually it works out pretty well, though. There's something I wanted to talk to you about." My father was sitting up straight on the sofa, his knees pressed tightly together.

"So how's married life treating you?" he asked. He was always throwing curve balls, this guy.

"Oh, we're coping."

"I see," he said, wrapping his hands around his coffee mug. He shifted uncomfortably in his chair. "Feels like a hospital in here."

"A hospital?"

"So empty and sterile. But that's just the modern style, I suppose."

Modern. I looked over at my father, trying to gauge the

meaning of what he had just said. But apparently he wasn't about to elaborate.

"How's Kon?"

"Fine," I said. "He comes by to visit from time to time."

"Here?"

"Yeah. More to see Shoko than me, though."

There was an uncomfortable moment of silence. My father smiled sadly. "Is that so?" he said. There was something tragic about his demeanor, a painful smile stuck resolutely on his face. I wished Shoko would hurry up and come back. Conversations with my father were always like this. Awkward and faltering. Had been for as long as I could remember. It always ended with him grinning awkwardly and me groping around for something—anything—to say.

"Shoko really likes Kon. She says they have a lot in common. Kon doesn't seem to mind her, either. You've seen the tree, right? Kon gave it to us as a wedding gift. *Yucca elephantipes* it's called. I can't remember if I pointed it out to you the last time you were here." I was chattering away inanely now, desperately trying to cover up the silence.

"Did you know that there are silver lions, Dad? They're born with almost no color—they're silver—and apparently they get rejected from the pride for being different from the other lions. So they go off somewhere far away and live in a group by themselves. Shoko told me about them. She says Kon and I remind her of the silver lions. They don't eat meat and they're not very strong and a lot of them die young. Lions that die young. Shoko has some pretty unique ideas, huh?" I laughed. God, what a washout this was turning out to be. Mother's lectures were far easier to deal with than this.

"I don't know about you guys," he said. He looked over at his babbling son and took a sip of coffee. "But as far as I can see, Shoko's a bit of a silver lion herself," he said, and let out another awkward laugh.

Just then, the phone rang. Thank God. Saved by the bell. I grabbed at the receiver, my salvation.

"Mutsuki?"

It was like hearing the voice of your beloved after a hundred years of separation.

"Where are you?"

Shoko ignored my question. "What should I get, *mizu-yokan* or *kuzuzakura*?

"What?"

She said it again.

"Either is fine." I really didn't care, but Shoko had gone silent on the other end of the phone, so I panicked and made a quick spur-of-the-moment decision.

"*Mizu-yokan*. It's got to be *mizu-yokan*. No doubt about it."

"Yeah, I thought so too," Shoko said, and we hung up.

Shoko's call gave me a bit of much needed time to get a grip on myself before I faced my father again. Now it was my turn to ask the questions. "How's Mother?" I said.

He blinked a few times before he replied. "Fine. Same as ever. You know what your mother's like."

I certainly did.

"Oh by the way, don't tell your mother I came to see you today." He said it looking at his coffee and with an ambiguous smile on his face.

"Okay."

"Shoko seems to be a good wife."

I concurred. He looked up at me for a moment, and then glanced back down at his coffee without saying a word. Silent accusation. I know, I know, I repeated silently to myself.

Just as things were starting to drag again, Shoko came home to the rescue. Hallelujah!

"I just stopped by to say hello," my father said. Shoko gave a deep formal bow.

"It's been so long since we've seen you. Is Mother well?"

Back to square one. I went into the kitchen to make some tea. Behind me, I could hear my father saying, "Well, I just thought I'd drop by and see how you were getting along." Who was making excuses now? "Oh no, don't put yourself to any trouble. I won't stay long. It's just that my wife was out, and I was feeling like a bit of a loose end at home all by myself."

Afternoon sunlight slanted in through the kitchen window.

On top of the sink, the little goldfish was swimming around in its glass bowl. It was cut off completely from the outside world, its red body gliding happily through the water. I felt cool and refreshed just looking at it.

We drank cups of green tea, ate Shoko's chilled *mizu-yokan* jelly, and chatted about nothing. The flu-bug that was going around this summer, the price of cherries.... The air itself was smoother now that Shoko was home. The sweet *mizu-yokan* was cool against my tongue. My father seemed shy and fidgety.

It was later on that evening that I found out what Shoko had meant by her mysterious allusions to Mizuho's "last will and testament." Apparently Mizuho's interrogation had failed to arrive at the truth.

"She and I are no longer on talking terms," Shoko said.

"What?" I flinched slightly. It was such a shock to hear her talk like that. "Why?"

Shoko refused to explain. They were no longer friends, and that was that, as far as she was concerned. "Look, this is between me and my friend, okay? It has nothing to do with you."

"Don't be childish," I said. I took a sip of the fizzy orange-flavored cocktail Shoko had made.

"The amusement park thing was mostly my fault anyway. Why should you and Mizuho stop being friends over that?"

Shoko didn't answer.

"You can't decide just like that to cut ties with your best friend."

Shoko was glaring at me, but still she said nothing. She sat in silence, glass in hand.

"Mizuho's just worried about you—"

"What was I supposed to tell her?" Shoko shot back calmly. "How was I supposed to explain why you invited Haneki? It's all too much trouble. Can't be bothered! I'm doing quite fine, and I'll be fine as long as I have you. Us. I won't miss Mizuho. I have Kon, and Dr. Kakii, and Dr. Kashibe," the determined Shoko announced. I remembered what my father had said: she too was like a silver lion.

"So can we please not talk about Mizuho anymore?" she continued, gulping down the rest of her drink with evident enjoyment. "Aren't you going to finish yours?"

Go ahead, I said, and she took my glass. She smiled, and sipped at it slowly.

"Hmm, it tastes good: curaçao, tonic water, and Mutsuki," she muttered to herself.

I stood up. "I'll go fill up the bath."

Perhaps it really meant nothing to Shoko. She was pretty simple in her own way. But sometimes I felt confused over her. Her unguarded words, her naïve, trusting glances and smiles. Feelings I thought I had little to do with. But how could she make such drastic decisions so casually? Slowly but surely, she was isolating herself from the world in which her parents, Mizuho, and all the people she had ever loved lived. I wondered if she even realized what she was doing.

"You're filling the bath?" Shoko's eyes sparkled mischievously. "Why don't we fill up the tub with cold water and put the goldfish in it? A goldfish swimming pool! We can keep a record of how many minutes it takes for it to swim from one end to the other. A progress report. Like they do with those flowers—morning glories or whatever they're called. Then we can see how much progress it makes over the summer."

"Pretty wacky."

"And a lot of fun!" Shoko was excited, but there was already something fleeting about her excitement. It was almost painful to watch.

I twisted the temperature control to Cold and turned on the tap. Water gushed into the tub with a roar. I could hear Shoko singing in the living room.

Come here, little goldfish
In your red bib so neat
Open your big eyes
And I'll give you a treat

Maybe it was better if I saw Mizuho about this. She deserved an explanation. Shoko's parents, too, for that matter. Things had gone far enough already.

"Mutsukiiii!" Shoko shouted. "You want to try some of this fish food? It's pretty gross and dry and stinky, but you can kind of feel what it's like to be a goldfish."

"No, I think I'll pass. Thanks," I said, wiping my feet with a towel. Another fifteen minutes and the tub would be full. I'll make a graph, I thought. So you could see at a glance what sort of progress the fish was making. It would be a gift to Shoko. I could picture it already: the goldfish in the bathtub, swimming gracefully through the cold water.

JULY, CREATURES FROM OUTER SPACE

• •

By the time I woke up, daylight was already streaming in
through the blinds, drawing striped patterns on the sheets. I
rolled over and kicked the bedcovers away, and slid my hands
under the pillow. Mutsuki had already left for work, and the bed
next to mine was neatly made up. I looked around the room.
Little particles of dust so small you'd never see them unless the
sunlight hit them. Nothing beats a lazy summer morning.

The air conditioning was whirring softly in the living room.
The room felt empty. Music was playing in the background: a
Frescobaldi organ piece. The goldfish was swimming in the
goldfish bowl, and there was a fresh salad waiting for me in the
refrigerator. The whole room was dazzlingly white, everything
in its proper place. I stood motionless for a while, my head still
kind of groggy. What was it that was making me feel so anxious
and ill-at-ease, in this perfect space that Mutsuki had prepared
specially for me?

I went back into the bedroom and opened the closet. I took

out Mutsuki's suits one by one, and looked at them closely. The room was still streaked with sunlight. I laid his clothes out on the bed, and tried to remember what Mutsuki looked like in them. I needed to reassure myself that he really did exist, that he really was my husband.

Out they all came, one after another: jackets, jeans, T-shirts, and two pairs of shoes. I had practically buried the bed in Mutsuki's clothes by the time I could relax again. I took a shower and ate the salad. It had lots of nice little red crispy radishes in it. If only Mutsuki would hurry up and come home. I looked up at the clock. It wasn't even eleven yet.

The doorbell rang. I opened the door to find Kon standing outside.

"Morning!" he said, a bright and cheerful expression on his face, like someone from another land. "What a great day, huh?" he said.

The intruder took off his shoes and stepped inside. He sank down deep into the sofa.

"Can I get you something to drink?" I said. What else could I do? I stood at his side like a waitress taking an order.

"Orange juice," he said straight away, as if he'd been waiting for me to ask. He smiled. He had obviously only just got out of bed, and his soft hair was still tousled from last night's sleep. "And make sure it's freshly squeezed—"

I was already over by the refrigerator, leaning down for a

carton of juice.

Sap-like juice oozed from the peel as I squeezed the oranges and made my hands sticky. I felt a sting as the juice seeped into my hangnails. I licked it off my fingertips; it tasted bitter.

"This is the life. Hanging around at home with the missus on your day off."

"Except that it's not a holiday. And I'm not your wife."

"Mmm, too bad." Kon grinned. "I wish I had a wife too."

It was obvious he didn't mean it. I laughed. I put some ice into a glass and poured his orange juice. "A wife? But she'd have to be a woman," I said.

I was surprised to see Kon look serious all of a sudden. "Yeah, I guess you're right. I've never heard of a man-wife. But it's not really 'men' I like anyway. It's Mutsuki," he said straight-forwardly, as if it were no big deal.

"Mm-hmm." My heart missed a beat. That's just the way I felt too.

"Hey, are these California oranges?" Kon asked as he glugged away at his tall glass of juice.

"Yes." I had no idea, but I nodded anyway.

Kon looked satisfied. "I thought so. The Florida ones just aren't as sweet."

It was Kon's idea to pay a visit to Mutsuki at the hospital. They'd been together for twelve years, Kon said, and he'd never once seen what sort of face Mutsuki wore during work. I hadn't either, I said.

"That clinches it," Kon declared with a matter-of-fact nod. "We're definitely going then."

"And besides, it'll be cool if his wife and his boyfriend visited him at the same time."

Whether it was cool or not was of no concern to me. What interested me was what Mutsuki looked like to his patients. I wanted to see his professional face.

The roads were pretty empty, and we had no problem changing buses. The red brick hospital building looked sleepy in the midday sun. We gave our names to the young nurse at reception, who directed us to the lobby. "Please have a seat," she said in a businesslike manner. Déjà vu. I felt sure I'd been through it all before.

Kon was giving the place a good once-over. "Not the most cheerful workplace in the world," he muttered to himself.

I scrutinized the line of people in the waiting room, trying to guess what they were doing there: this one's waiting to be admitted, that one's just visiting. It was easy to spot the patients. They were all wearing hospital gowns. And they all had the same vacant expression on their faces.

"I'm afraid Dr. Kishida is not here at the moment." An older nurse, not the one we had talked to before, pattered over towards us. "He should be back in about an hour or so. Would you like to wait for him, or would you prefer to leave a message?"

She stared at us unblinkingly.

"We'll wait," said Kon, clearly and firmly.

"As you wish," the nurse replied. She didn't sound very pleased.

"Excuse me, nurse?" Kon stopped her as she started to walk away. "How about that nice dime-novel doctor in gynecology?"

"I beg your pardon?"

The nurse shot us a really suspicious look, but Kon chirruped on regardless. "Dr. Daisuke Kakii. Is he available?"

This seemed to make the nurse more suspicious of us than ever. "One minute please," she said, and shuffled back to reception. We stayed where we were on the sofa, a couple of unwelcome guests.

Before long, I saw Dr. Kakii stepping lightly down the corridor towards us, his eyes blinking like crazy behind his thick glasses. "Hello. Anything wrong? It's not often we see you here at the hospital."

And with Kon too, he seemed to be implying. He didn't seem very pleased to see us either. I told him we were here to see what Mutsuki did at work. How do we get to the elderly ward, I asked him.

"Third floor. But you can't go into any of the sickrooms," Dr. Kakii said, walking ahead of us. "And none of your little pranks. Nothing at all. Is that clear?"

Kon glared at Dr. Kakii. "What do you think I am? As if I'm going to start picking on a bunch of sick old people. I'm not some naughty little school kid out on a field trip, okay? So spare me the lecture."

"I'm sorry. I didn't mean it like that. I just wanted to make things clear, just in case...." Dr. Kakii was all flustered. His face was a bright red.

The elevator reached the third floor.

We followed Dr. Kakii down the corridor through the ward. I was starting to feel really nervous and out of place. There were old people everywhere. Old men in *yukata* robes watching TV in the waiting room; balding old ladies inching their way painfully down the hallway, clutching on to the handrail for support. The place was overflowing with old people, and the whole floor had a distinctive ambience. I could tell that Kon had tensed up too, but Dr. Kakii was still marching along as briskly as ever, and we had to walk fast to keep up.

"Most of the patients in this room are under Mutsuki's care," he said. The room was much bigger than I'd expected. There were four rows of beds, five beds in each row, all lined up in orderly fashion.

"Wow."

Some of the patients were having lunch, with the help of a nurse. The nurses were all surprisingly cheerful, speaking in loud clear voices as they spooned rice gruel into the patients' mouths.

"Open wide, that's it. Hmm, very good! One more time. O-pen wi-ide."

For every obedient old man opening his mouth as he was told, there was an old woman weakly shaking her head and refusing her food. And for every old woman asking for pickled radishes or more tea, there was an old man yelling in a robust voice that he wasn't ready to eat yet. Still the nurses' cheerful tone never faltered.

"Here we go, open wide. Hmm, isn't that delicious? O-pen wi-ide."

We stood in the doorway and stared in disbelief at the scene before our eyes.

"Lunch starts at eleven, but on this ward it can be anything up to two hours before everyone's done," Dr. Kakii said flatly.

"Is this your grandson, pop?"

Kon had struck up a conversation with a promising-looking old man who had refused his lunch.

"I knew it. He's up to something," Dr. Kakii said painfully. I had to laugh to myself.

"Son," the old man said, glancing over at the photo near his bed. "My son. That's my son."

It was a color photograph of a little baby.

Gesturing toward Kon with her chin, an old lady in the bed

next to his asked him, "Really? This is your son?"

"Yup. He's my son, too."

Things were getting out of hand. Kon didn't bother to argue.

"You must be his daughter," the old lady said, turning to me.

"That's right. She's my little sister," Kon said.

Little sister! I was seething inside, but Kon and the old lady were grinning away quite happily at each other. Two of her front teeth were missing.

"Well that *is* nice. What a nice brother and sister."

I muttered some vague, noncommittal response. "What a nice brother and sister." He could at least have said I was his *older* sister.

A plastic bamboo branch hung from the end of the old lady's bed, not far from the close-cropped head that peeked out from under the sheets. Attached to the bamboo was a piece of origami paper.

"Tanabata!" I said suddenly, without thinking. The day after tomorrow was the Tanabata festival. I had forgotten all about it.

"One of my grandchildren brought it in for me," she said proudly. She flashed me a grin, and I could see the gaps in her teeth again.

"Come on you two. That's enough," Dr. Kakii prompted us. He certainly looked as if he had had enough. I turned around for a last look as we left the room. The old lady was already lying on her side and the old man was staring after us with an unsettling poker face. I left feeling half-heartedly sympathetic.

"That's the last time I ever take you at your word, Kon. I was right to worry about letting you come up here. I take back what I said before about being sorry." Dr. Kakii sped down the hallway, his face turning a bright red again.

By the time we got to the doctors' offices, Mutsuki was back. He obviously couldn't believe his eyes when he saw Kon and me being escorted down the corridor by Dr. Kakii.

"What's going on?" he said.

"They're your responsibility now," Dr. Kakii grumped and left the three of us alone.

Mutsuki made us some coffee. I breathed in its soothing fragrance, and felt its warmth surge through my body. There's something about hospitals that always scares me.

"So what do those people have?" I asked.

"What people?"

"Those people on the third floor in that huge room. Dr. Kakii gave us a tour. I hope you don't mind."

Sipping his coffee, Mutsuki said he didn't. "I don't suppose there's anything particularly wrong with them. Little things. Weak heart, kidney problems. It's only to be expected at that age."

"Then why are they in a hospital?"

Mutsuki looked down into his coffee for a moment, silent.

"Oh, a variety of factors."

A variety of factors.

"Those nurses reminded me of schoolteachers. It kind of freaked me out."

"Hey, don't you have to go on your rounds?" Kon asked. "We came specifically to see Dr. Kishida at work. Where were you until now, anyway?"

It was Kon who had asked the question, but Mutsuki looked at me as he answered. "I was at lunch. I went out."

Oh, I said. Weird Mutsuki. Why was he bothering to explain himself to me? Where he ate his lunch was his own business.

Mutsuki's next rounds weren't until the evening, and he had a meeting at two, so Kon and I decided to call it a day. Besides, I felt like I had seen Mutsuki at work. In fact, we had known all along what he looked like to his patients.

Mutsuki walked us as far as the main entrance.

"Take care getting home. Remember, it's the #6 bus you want, and then you change to the #1 in front of the big office building."

Blinding sunlight flashed off the stone steps as we walked away from the hospital. Mutsuki stood in front of the sliding doors, his hands in his pockets. His white coat was bright and clean, like something out of a TV commercial for laundry detergent. The building looked as tired as ever. I gazed up at the windows on the third floor.

"They're from outer space," Kon said at my side. He was also looking up at the third floor.

After I got off the bus and said bye to Kon, I decided to drop by a convenience store to buy some origami paper. I sat down with a can of beer as soon as I arrived home, and got to work on Tanabata decorations. I made rings and chains, and cut the paper into all kinds of shapes and patterns. One sheet I folded into the shape of a bellows and made a paper lantern. Then I wrote out my wishes—lots of them. That my Italian would improve, that the editor would forget my deadlines, that I would grow five centimeters taller. I left the last strip of paper blank, and just tied it with a piece of string. The most important wish had to be a secret; that was the best way of making sure it came true. When I'd finished all the decorations I hung them on Kon's tree. The mess I'd made lay scattered all around me: bits of paper, the lid to the bottle of glue, a few empty beer cans, a pair of scissors. Kon's tree was way too big for the job, really, compared to the delicate little bamboo branch you were supposed to use. It looked kind of shy about being the center of attention all of a sudden. But you could tell it was feeling proud and happy at the same time. I dragged Kon's tree out onto the veranda.

I felt a sudden craving for *edamame* string beans. I stepped out to the local grocer's and bought a whole bunch of them. After about five minutes on the boil, they were a beautiful bright green. I flipped them out onto a sieve and sprinkled salt over them. Mutsuki would be home any minute. It was getting dark. Out on the veranda, the paper decorations looked ready to melt away into the ink-black night.

Mutsuki came back from work and slid open the glass door. He laughed out loud. "That tree looks embarrassed."

It really did. Stiff, awkward, sulky, and embarrassed. It was a pretty clumsy tree. Out on the veranda, Mutsuki and I sat drinking beer and eating *edamame*, and saying nice things about Kon's tree. It was a pretty great tree, we both agreed. It was sturdy, it didn't attract bugs, and in a pinch it could stand in as a Tanabata bamboo. What more could anyone want from a tree?

"Let's have dinner out here," I said. Mutsuki smiled and nodded. Good idea, he said.

"How about some cold noodles? Nice and refreshing."

"Sounds good," he nodded again.

"Mutsuki?" I didn't know why, but suddenly I felt uneasy. The calm expression on Mutsuki's face made him seem so far away. "What are you thinking about?"

"Nothing," he said. He was staring straight at the moon, which shone like a huge white ball in the sky. He smiled sadly, further unsettling me.

But even so, he seemed to be in an unusually good mood. He ate a good-sized helping of noodles, and even had ice cream for dessert (he rarely had dessert). For once, he was the one to suggest we have a drink, and he made mint juleps for us both. He seemed genuinely to like my decorations and lavished praise on them. He was sure he couldn't find better decorations in all of Japan.

"Mutsuki?"

"What?" He looked over at me with his gentle, faraway eyes—eyes which seemed to tell me that no matter what I did, they would always be forgiving.

"Why don't you write down your wishes, too?" I said cheerfully, handing him some origami paper. "You're allowed up to three wishes. I made a lot more, though."

"No, thanks." Mutsuki folded his arms in front of his chest. "I don't have any. I'm happy with things just the way they are."

I stood up and put my glass on the floor.

"Shoko?"

I ignored Mutsuki's worried look and scrounged around for the piece of paper I hadn't written on earlier. It was a light blue color, at the top of the tree.

"Let's write our names on it," I said. I got out a thick felt-tipped pen and wrote both our names. Mutsuki looked unconvinced.

"You know what I wished for?" I said. "I wished that we could stay like this forever. That's what this piece of paper was for. But I thought if I wrote it down, it wouldn't come true, so I left it blank."

I fell silent. Mutsuki looked sad. No, more pained than sad. Like he couldn't take it much longer.

"What's wrong?" I managed to say at last.

"But things *can't* stay the same," Mutsuki said, finally finding his voice. "Time flows, people come and go. It's inevitable. Things change."

This I couldn't accept. "Why are you talking like that all of a sudden? You said we could stay like this forever. If we both want this, why can't it go on?"

"Shoko," he said calmly but firmly, "I went to see Mizuho today. I explained everything to her. The amusement park thing, everything."

There was a long moment of silence before I said anything.

"Huh?"

"I explained everything." Mutsuki was very calm. He was looking straight at me.

"You're kidding." I struggled to make sense of what was going on, but my head was a void. This wasn't happening. It couldn't be true. Then for some reason, the faces of the old people came back to me like snapshots. Time flows, people come and go.

"You asshole." I was surprised by how weak my voice sounded. Underneath the diamond-studded sky, the paper chain that decorated Kon's tree was flapping and fluttering in the breeze.

FAMILY CONFERENCE

• •

I parked the car next to my father-in-law's sedan. I'd always known it would come to this one day. At that point I felt more relieved than anything else by the sight of his white Mark II in the parking lot. I had waited two weeks. Mizuho was at a loss. She was truly shaken up by the latest developments. She kept trying to call, but Shoko refused to pick up the phone. "We're not friends anymore. I want nothing to do with her," she would say, and that was the end of that. It was up to Shoko to make the call, not me. All I would do was make things worse and end up hurting them both. My feet felt heavy as I stepped out of the elevator.

Shoko had hardly spoken to me since that day. "How could you be so *stupid*?" she'd screamed at me. "How could you go and tell Mizuho everything like that?" But what else did she want me to do? The very fact that she was making all those desperate wishes for things to remain as they were meant that deep down she knew as well as I did that we couldn't go on like that.

Mizuho's reaction two weeks earlier when I'd told her how things stood was a perfectly reasonable one. We had lunch at a family restaurant near the hospital. At first, she was speechless. "Are you kidding me?" she'd said at last with a smile. But there was no sign of mirth in her eyes, and it didn't take her long to see that I was absolutely serious. Shyly, she pushed me for more details, still struggling to believe what she was hearing. Why did I agree to a meeting in the first place? Did Shoko's parents know about any of this? And all the time, she kept muttering: "Well, I don't know about that," or, "But that's just ridiculous."

I answered all her questions honestly. I told her I was used to meeting with potential marriage partners—to put Mother at ease—and that I had intended my relationship with Shoko to go no further than that first formal meeting. I recounted what a foul mood Shoko had been in that day.

She hadn't smiled once the whole time. She'd been wearing a new white dress, but with her entire body she was sending messages that she didn't want to be wearing it at all. She had a scowl on her face the whole time. Not that she seemed angry or irritable, she was more like a small animal cornered for the kill. Something about it really got to me. Her wide open eyes reminded me of Kon's. I waited for the go-between to make the announcement that it was time "for the young couple to be left to themselves," according to the rules of the game.

The first thing I said when we were alone was, "This is going to sound horribly rude, but I'm afraid I have no intention of getting married."

Shoko looked at me fixedly for a while and then said, "That's funny. Neither do I."

Mizuho interrupted me at that point. "Well then, why?" It wasn't so much a question. More like a bitter accusation. The *macaroni au gratin* she had ordered was still sitting in front of her hardly touched. She sighed. "I really wish you hadn't told me all this," her face seemed to say.

My father-in-law was waiting for me in the living room, puffing heavily on a cigarette. The ashtray he had brought in with him from the car was already full of butts.

"Hello. Thanks for stopping by," I said with a bow.

He nodded and stubbed out his half-smoked cigarette. His thin smile bore little resemblance to the kind, friendly expression I was used to seeing on his face.

"Shoko's in the washroom."

The washroom? Suddenly I was worried about her, but as soon as I began to move my father-in-law stopped me. "There's something I want to talk to you about first. It won't take long. Sit down."

"Let me make you some tea," I said, but he was in no mood for formalities or small-talk.

"No. I want to talk."

There was no escape. I braced myself and sat down opposite him.

"Mizuho came by to see me at work today," he began. "She told me some of the things you had discussed with her and, well, frankly, I'm in a state of shock." He paused and studied me closely. "It's not true, is it?" He was wearing a short-sleeved white shirt and gray pants. He was a little on the stout side. He had started to lose his hair, and was wearing glasses with black frames.

"It's true," I said, staring back at his glasses.

"Now wait a minute. That can't be right." He was upset. "What I'm trying to get at is—and don't take this the wrong way—is...are...you a homosexual?"

He got up from the sofa. He was so agitated he couldn't remain seated. "This was an arranged marriage, for God's sake! I don't remember seeing anything about this in your personal file, on your health forms. I mean, are you seriously trying to tell me that my own son-in-law is not—*not a real man*? It's pre-posterous! You don't expect me to believe that, do you?"

After that, he oscillated between angry denunciations and whispered pleas. Shortly after drawing himself up magisterially to yell at me that I was an impostor, he would weakly whisper, "No, no, no, please...." A fine young man like me! I couldn't possibly be a *homo*!

I said nothing. I could hear the hum of the refrigerator in the kitchen. My father-in-law sat back down on the sofa and hung his head. He looked inconsolable. For a long while, neither of us moved.

"I'm leaving." Suddenly he stood up and put on his jacket, and marched off without even looking at me. As he put on his shoes in the hallway, I heard him muttering, "What am I supposed to tell my wife?" I saw him off in silence, my head held low. The door slammed, and a heavy metallic thud echoed through the hall.

"Hi, Shoko, I'm home." I thought I ought to speak to her. "Your father just left."

"Oh?" Shoko said, staring at the tub. The white sheet with the graph on it was hanging in a folder by the side of the sink. But the bathtub was too large for there to be improving time records. The goldfish hadn't once made it across.

"You think he'll make it today?" I asked, but Shoko didn't respond. Not much hope. The fish drifted motionless in the water.

"If you're an imposter," Shoko said, staring at the fish, "then I'm an imposter too. Isn't that so?" She looked serious, her brows knitted together. "My dad just doesn't get it at all."

She was trying to cheer me up. Suddenly I felt forlorn. I stood staring at Shoko's back. Her long hair, her narrow shoulders, her slightly calloused heels.

We had a phone call from my father-in-law later that

evening. He was going to come and see us on Sunday, he said. "With my wife," he added. He was calmer than before, but his voice was still brimming with anger.

"And I'd appreciate it if your parents were there, too. Make sure Shoko knows."

I assured him I would tell her, but there was no need. Shoko was standing right next to me with her ear pressed to the phone, holding her breath, a frown on her face.

"Yes, of course. The day after tomorrow then. After lunch. Yes, we'll be here." I hung up, and Shoko ripped out the cord. "I guess we can have a bit of peace and quiet tomorrow," she said.

Sunday came all too quickly. Shoko wore a pokerface at breakfast, eating a noodle salad that she had prepared herself. I had completely lost my appetite. I drank three cups of coffee, and looked through the papers. I polished the pans to try and calm myself down. It was beautiful weather outside. In the apartment building opposite ours, a woman was hanging her futon out on the balcony to air.

My parents arrived at eleven o'clock, two hours early. Mother took off her high heels and placed them neatly by the door. Isn't it hot today, she said as we sat down in the living room.

"I'm glad we got here first," she said.

They were obviously tense, but to my relief they seemed

much calmer than I'd expected. "And how are you, Shoko?" she said, her red lips breaking into a smile as she handed over the small package she'd brought with her. "These are for you," she said, scrunching her nose as she smiled. "Plums. I hope you like them." Yes, thank you, Shoko said, smiling back. It was an awkward smile.

"We were so surprised when we heard they wanted to see us so suddenly. We tried calling you yesterday, but we couldn't get through. I wonder what it is they have to say, getting us all together like this," Mother said, taking a small fan from her handbag. The scent of sandalwood mixed with the sweet smell of her perfume.

"Why don't we just wait until they get here," my father interrupted, but Mother just ignored him. Shoko set down glasses of barley tea on the table.

"I'm not surprised your parents were so shocked. I feel terrible about it myself," Mother said, theatrically letting her shoulders sag. "But your marriage is your own business after all, and nobody else's," she proclaimed. "You knew about Kon when you married Mutsuki, didn't you, Shoko? What matters is the way you two feel about each other, no? People can say what they like, you're both grown-ups. You can make up your own minds."

The way she was talking astounded me. This was not good. If she carried on like this we'd be lucky if any of us survived the impending catastrophe.

Shoko's parents arrived at one on the dot. Suddenly every-thing became tense.

"Hey, a family conference," Shoko whispered to me. I guess it was funny. Our parents sat together around our small table, scowling at one another silently over glasses of barley tea. It was my father-in-law who spoke first.

"We want an explanation," he said. "What were you thinking when you arranged for your son to get married? I take it you were aware of his tendency...his proclivity...."

But Mother was ready for this, and she responded with her theory of Love Conquers Everything. "We were against it, of course. But they were so determined, you see. And we thought, if Mutsuki and Shoko really love each other that much, then all we can do, really, is to be as supportive as we possibly can." She paused for effect, and then went on cheerfully, "After all, they're young and have a whole future ahead of them."

Not bad, Mother!

"Be that as it may, I still think you should have consulted us first."

"You're right," my father said, bowing his head. "We're terri-bly sorry."

Shoko raised her eyebrows, but didn't say a word.

"But what upsets me more than anything is that *our own daughter* didn't tell us anything." My mother-in-law started to sniffle.

Much to my annoyance, Mother was soon dabbing at her eyes as well. "I know, I know. I understand how you must feel."

And so it went on. Shoko and I seemed to be surplus to requirements, excluded from their cozy little circle.

"I still can't believe it." My father-in-law's face was full of pent-up resentment.

Shoko spoke up nonchalantly. "Well, we're both at fault, you know. We're both hiding something."

Well, that was that. There was no way Mother was going to pass up an opportunity like that one, and in the end we had to let them see the two medical forms we kept in the top drawer of the bedroom dresser: the mental health certificate that declared Shoko's mental illness to be "nothing abnormal," and the results of my AIDS test, which showed me to be HIV negative. Both sets of parents looked on with breathless interest.

"This is no joke," Mother said. Suddenly, she was furious. "Homosexuality is a question of personal preference, but mental illness! Mental illness is hereditary."

"Personal preference? I can't believe what I'm hearing," my father-in-law said. "He's not a real man. He is a man-woman. People like him shouldn't be allowed to get married. And Shoko's emotional instability is just a temporary thing. I mean these days everybody in Europe and America is in therapy."

I couldn't get a word in edgewise. Shoko was sitting drinking her barley tea, her face blank and expressionless. But I was sure she was as sick of all this as I was.

I had to say something. "Actually, you know, we like it this way."

"*Sì, sì,*" Shoko agreed loudly with me.

There was a moment's silence, and then my father-in-law asked quite calmly, "And I take it you'll be breaking things off with your, boyfriend, am I right?"

I knew this question was going to come up at some stage, and I had an answer ready. Yes, I will break things off. That was what I was going to say. But I couldn't get the words out. Kon's back and the smell of coke filled my mind.

"If Mutsuki leaves Kon," Shoko said, standing by me, "then I'm leaving Mutsuki."

This stunned everyone into silence.

It was a stormy afternoon. In the end, the meeting broke up without reaching any consensus (as if such a thing were possible), leaving us only with bottomless exhaustion.

"Here." Shoko held her cup to my face. I took a sip. It wasn't tea at all, but whiskey. No doubt about it. She'd been drinking whiskey on the rocks the whole time. Ha ha ha. Shoko giggled with delight. The woman on the balcony opposite was beating the dust out of her futon.

"Say you don't regret it," Shoko said, sipping her whiskey.

"...It's like your dad said I guess. People like me just should-n't get married."

Shoko looked at me in surprise. Her big eyes flashed with anger. "Are you stupid?" she spat out. Her face turned bright red, she glared at me for a few seconds, and I thought she was about to start crying. She got up and walked out of the room, leaving me alone with the Tree of Youth and the Cézanne.

I found Shoko in the bedroom, flat out on her bed in tears, just as I had expected. When my wife cries, she really cries. I sat down next to her and said I was sorry. She was hugging her pillow close, determined not to look up.

"I don't regret it. Of course I don't regret it," I said.

I had to look the other way. It was always this way with Shoko: straightforward expressions of simple, naked emotion. Did I really deserve to be loved like this?

"Shall we have some champagne?"

Her crying quieted down. Her face still buried in the pillow, Shoko nodded. We had used up all the money set aside for groceries this month, so I made a mountain of *okonomiyaki* flour cakes with cabbage for dinner. Before long, the room was full of smoke, and you could smell the burnt sauce. We drank the fake champagne and wolfed down the *okonomiyaki*.

"You want to invite Kon over?" Shoko suggested, tilting her head slightly. Her eyes were red and swollen. "I really miss him."

Before I even had time to agree, Shoko picked up the phone. I plugged the cord back into the jack.

"Hi, Kon? It's Shoko."

I went out on the veranda. I looked in through the glass doors to the brightly lit room inside. Shoko was chatting away happily on the phone. Since when had those two been so close anyway? A pale crescent moon hung in the sky.

Kon appeared in less than an hour, lugging a watermelon with him.

"God, it's so humid! It's like the tropics, Shoko."

"You want me to squeeze you some California orange juice?" Shoko asked.

"You got it," Kon said.

"Go wash your hands," I said, "I'll get the hotplate ready."

"Shrimp and pig ball *okonomiyaki* for me," he said. You could always rely on Kon to lower the level of a conversation.

Shoko was squeezing oranges in the kitchen.

"You want me to do it?" I said. She shook her head. Three oranges were sliced in half on the chopping board. They all had green stamps on them saying "FLORIDA."

"I'm gonna go ahead and eat!" Kon called from the living room. He was sitting with one knee up at the table.

It was a fun evening. After dinner, we sat around eating the watermelon and the plums and playing games. Then we went in and did the dishes together. Shoko, who was in unusually high spirits, just wouldn't let Kon go home. "Oh please stay! You can't go home yet."

"What about that new CD you just bought, Mutsuki? Let's

listen to it. Come on."

And so we listened to Schubert's "Fantasia" over coffee. As soon as the music started, Shoko and Kon both fell silent.

"Can we turn off the lights?" Kon asked.

Why is it that everything sounds so much clearer in the dark? The evening sky was the color of plums. It was even darker inside the apartment. We stretched out our legs on the floor and listened as piano music filled the room. Quick, pure notes. The crescent moon spread its cold light slowly across the nighttime sky.

When I turned the lights back on and looked at my watch, it was past one in the morning. Shoko stood up and said she was going to call it a night, and went into the bedroom.

"Shoko-chan's so cute," Kon said. "She saw you looking at your watch. That's why she went off to bed."

But I didn't need him to tell me. I already knew. "Come on, I'll drive you home," I said.

The car drove straight on through the night. I knew exactly how Shoko felt when she said she really needed to see Kon tonight.

It had been a long day. Memories came back to me: the strident tone of Mother's voice, my father-in-law's angry glare, the pattern on my mother-in-law's tear-stained handkerchief, my father with his head drooping. I don't regret a thing, I said to

Shoko in my heart.

Kon wasted no time making himself comfortable. He tipped the seat back and was soon fast asleep, his mouth half-open.

"You're a funny one," I said.

But the truth was that I had really missed Kon, too. I put my hand on his thigh, and then drew it back again immediately. I felt foolish, and laughed at myself. Suddenly, I felt incredibly lonely. High up above us, the crescent moon still hung suspended in the sky.

THE STAR-SOWER

• •

It was becoming increasingly clear that honesty was an extremely important concept for Mutsuki. Apparently there was nothing he wouldn't go through for the sake of honesty. Even an ordeal like that stupid family conference. But to make up for it, I was becoming more and more dishonest all the time. I was betraying everybody: both sets of parents, Mizuho, and probably Mutsuki's conscience too. What had happened to make everything so complicated? I wanted to protect the life I had with Mutsuki. To think that, when we started out, we practically had nothing to lose! Until I met Mutsuki, it never occurred to me to fight for anything.

That morning, I went in to talk to Dr. Kakii about artificial insemination. I arrived at the appointed time, handed over my health insurance details, and completed the form they make you fill out on your first visit. At the top of the piece of paper were the words "Obstetrics * Gynecology" written in thick green ink. They seemed unusually vivid, almost physical, as if I were seeing them for the first time.

The nurse called out my name and held open the door to the doctor's office.

"Oh, it's you!" Dr. Kakii looked at me in surprise. "Are you here for a check-up?" he asked curiously. "Or...is something the matter?" He was speaking formally enough, but it didn't really feel like a visit to the doctor's. He just didn't seem much like a doctor, somehow.

"I wanted to ask for advice. It's about artificial insemination."

Dr. Kakii stiffened. "Erm, well, wait a minute," he stuttered. "Wouldn't you rather discuss this over lunch?" He was flustered.

"Sorry, there's somewhere I have to go right after this," I said. He had no choice now. I'd made an appointment to see him, I'd even brought my insurance card, and I had come all this way. After all that, I wasn't going to let him just brush me off.

I was shown into a small examination room. There was a lighting instrument that looked like a machine for boiling eggs, an examination table with stirrups attached to it, a stool, and a bidet.

"You don't really have to give me an exam, you know," I said.

Dr. Kakii laughed a little when he saw me flinch. "Don't worry," he said. "This way the nurse won't hear us."

I had forgotten that this was Mutsuki's hospital too. I felt ashamed of my own carelessness. I had even written "Shoko Kishida" on the outpatient form. Even if I wasn't a regular patient, I could hardly pretend that I had no connection to Mutsuki.

"All right then." Dr. Kakii pushed up his glasses with the back of his right hand. "You say you want to know more about artificial insemination, is that right?"

For the time it took him to explain things to me, Dr. Kakii was a different person. He didn't fidget or bite his nails. He spoke in a calm manner—like a real doctor—balancing warmth with professional distance. I was pretty impressed by the sudden transformation.

The only problem was that what he had to say was really boring. He didn't discuss any of the stuff I really wanted to know about: what happened exactly, how it was done, how much it cost. He was like a school principal at morning assembly, droning on and on and on. He kept talking about all those picky little details: the Code of Ethical Standards issued by the Japanese Gynecological Association ("It's not law, so it's not exactly compulsory," he said, "but according to these standards, a doctor is supposed to perform the operation only on a woman who has no hope of becoming pregnant by any other means"); the considered medical opinion of the American Infertility Association; British government guidelines; and a whole bunch of other stuff I really didn't care about at all. I waited as patiently as I could for Dr. Kakii to come to the end of his lecture and then had to ask him a long series of questions to find out what I really wanted to know. Things much more practical (and important) than any Code of Ethical Standards.

Dr. Kakii responded seriously to all my questions. He did tend to rush over some of the most important points, but at the very least it was a useful lesson in medical jargon.

"But however you look at it," Dr. Kakii said, more to put an end to my questions than because he was drawing to a conclusion, "the first thing you should do is talk this over with Mutsuki."

I stopped by my parents' on the way home from the hospital. Today's main event. I walked uphill along the gently sloping road I knew so well. The big white house on the right, the thick hedge of fragrant olives on the left. I passed the house with the dog, turned right by the big apartment building, and there it was: the house I'd called home for more than twenty years, with its light brown walls and blue-tiled roof. The house where I grew up. The heavy russet gates, the faded wooden nameplate you could barely make out. I pressed the buzzer. My mom was always telling me not to bother, to come straight in, but I couldn't help it. It never really occurred to me that there was any other way to enter.

"Hello?" Her muffled voice came through the intercom.

"It's me, Shoko," I said.

I stretched my legs in front of me on the tatami mat and looked out at the persimmon tree in the garden as I sipped my tea. It was a quiet, sunny afternoon.

"You could have let us know you were coming," my mom said, peeling a pear in the kitchen. "There's nothing to eat. If I'd known you were coming, I would have bought something. Your father won't be back until late tonight. He would have come home early if he'd known you were coming."

I knew he'd be out. That was the whole reason I'd decided to come on a Monday. My dad's big theory was that it was best to go out drinking on Monday nights since everywhere was so packed on Fridays. The poor guys who worked for my dad always ended up having to take antacids right at the start of the week.

"I came by to give you the news," I said, standing in a corner of the kitchen. "Mutsuki broke up with his boyfriend."

My mom stopped what she was doing and put down her knife. She looked at me with a mixture of hope and doubt. "Really?" she said.

I summoned up the most inscrutable expression I could manage, and nodded seriously. "I told him he didn't have to, but I think he wanted a fresh start. You know, a normal family life, normal kids, all that stuff."

"...Normal kids...and stuff?" My mom looked suspicious.

"Yeah, you know, I think he wanted to start doing all the normal things that normal couples do."

My mom was quiet for a moment. And then she laughed like a girl. "How funny!"

I tried to laugh too, but it was all so bizarre that my laugh came out sounding hollow. "I thought you'd be pleased. That's why I came over to tell you." I said it resentfully, and mom finally believed me. Her pretty eyes, with their long thin lashes, were sparkling with delight.

"Well!" she exclaimed, and then fell silent. Tears came to her eyes. "That's good. That's wonderful news. We were so worried. Your father will be so pleased."

Perfect. Everything was going according to plan. She was so trusting.

"We have to let him know right away." She started towards the phone in the hall.

"Surely it can wait until he gets home?" I said, but she ignored me and picked up the receiver.

"What are you talking about? We have to let him know at once."

I had a bad feeling about this.

My mom bubbled excitedly into the phone for about five minutes. "It's true. If you could see her, you'd know it's true. Mother's instinct. Well, come home and see for yourself then. Yes, yes I know, but really, you shouldn't doubt your own daughter like that, poor girl." She was talking less excitedly now. "No, just Shoko. I don't know, he must be at work. It's the middle of the afternoon. I know, but Shoko wanted to let us know as soon as possible. What? Hmm. All right, then. Yes, hold on a minute." My mom put her hand over the receiver and turned towards me. "Is Mutsuki coming over later?"

I shook my head. "He's on the night shift."

Her expression clouded over slightly at this. "Your father says Mutsuki should come and talk to us himself, face to face. I agree with your father, but if Mutsuki has to work tonight then I don't suppose there's much we can do about it. What about tomorrow? I mean, he *is* going to come by one of these days, right?"

There was nothing I could do but nod yes.

By the time I got home I was exhausted. I opened a window to let the breeze in and made myself a drink. Pimms and ginger ale. I didn't want to drag Mutsuki into this if I could help it, but now that it had come to this I had no choice but to ask him to play along. It would only be for one evening anyway. I climbed in under the clean white sheets and rolled over onto my stomach, looking out across the veranda at the evening sky. The pillows felt cold against my cheek. I closed my eyes and listened carefully. That safe, warm, cozy feeling everywhere. It was like being in Mutsuki's arms, lying here like this. I stayed like that for a while, quite still. It was such a nice, kind room. The walls, the windows, the ceiling, the bed, they were all watching out for me. I knew it with my eyes closed. I could feel it. This was my haven.

I was dozing on the bed when Mutsuki came home. I woke up when he put a blanket over me. It was already dark.

"Welcome home," I said, still half-asleep.

Mutsuki smiled. "Hi. I got us some croquettes."

Now that he mentioned it, I thought I could smell them.

Over dinner, I introduced the idea of having kids. "I think it would be nice to have one, at least."

Mutsuki looked at me strangely. "What are you talking about, all of a sudden?"

"I talked to Dr. Kakii today. He says the fertility rates are really high with frozen insemination. Apparently it's best to have it done while you're still young. After forty, the success rate drops sharply, to about 3-7%."

"Forty? But that's thirteen years away."

"That's true," I faltered. "But your mother might finally approve of me if we have a baby."

Mutsuki said nothing. He had a stern look on his face. "You realize, of course, that once you've had a child you have to bring it up. I mean, it's not like having a pet dog. You can't just get rid of it when you get bored of it or when things get difficult."

"That's not a very nice thing to say about dogs."

Mutsuki sighed. "All I'm saying is that having a baby is serious business. You can't enter into it casually. And you shouldn't worry so much about what Mother thinks."

Now it was my turn to sigh. "Somewhere along the line, we're going to have to come to terms with the facts," I said.

I made the after-dinner tea. We were well into our second cup before either of us said a word.

"Do you have any plans for tomorrow night? My parents asked us to dinner."

Mutsuki looked surprised. They hadn't been in touch since the night the family meeting ended. "What's the catch?"

I told him about my visit that afternoon, and about how my mother had been so excited by my story that she'd insisted on calling my dad right away. "Look, it'll be really easy. Just stop by on your way home from the hospital tomorrow. We'll have dinner with them and you can just tell them what they want to hear. If you say you and Kon broke up, that should be good enough." I tried to make it sound like it was no big deal.

"But Shoko." I could tell there was something serious coming. "That wouldn't be true. There's no way I could lie like that to your parents."

"Oh god, Mutsuki, not again." I felt my strength slipping away. "You're so indecisive." It was supposed to have been an accusation, but all that came out was a feeble-sounding whisper. "Please? Just this once?"

Mutsuki looked at me sadly, without making any reply. Please, I said again, but still Mutsuki didn't answer.

By the time I realized what I was doing, I had thrown everything I could lay my hands on at Mutsuki. Teapot. Tea strainer. CDs. Watering can. Tea cozy. Mints. Paperbacks. My tears were flowing freely now, as I hurled one thing after another in his direction. I could hear myself bawling. He was like a little hedgehog, his honesty standing up on end like tiny prickles. He wasn't afraid to speak the truth. I was scared to death of it, of course. As far as I understood, words weren't there for telling the truth. I felt heartbroken. Why had I ever gotten married? Why did I have to like Mutsuki so much?

"Shoko!" Mutsuki put his arms around me from behind, as if he were holding a child. I realized that I was shaking. I couldn't control myself. My sobs were coming louder and louder. I couldn't live without Mutsuki anymore.

"It's all right. Calm down. Everything's okay." Slowly, Mutsuki smoothed away the strands of hair that were stuck to my face with my tears and sweat. The gentle touch of his large, dry palm. I felt terrible. I twisted in his arms.

"Shoko?"

Maybe it meant nothing to someone as good as Mutsuki. Perhaps for him it was all just kindness, and friendship, and family obligations. But I was different. Sometimes the pain got so bad I couldn't take it anymore. My whole body felt like some sorry piece of fruit. The palm of his hand stroking my hair, his fingertips as he fastened my earrings for me—the slightest little things tortured me.

"Let me go. I'm fine."

What I couldn't stand was not that I couldn't sleep with Mutsuki, but that Mutsuki was so calm and kind about everything. The feeling I had that I was embracing water came not from the loneliness of a sexless marriage, but from the complex we both had about it—the suffocating need to be sensitive to the other's feelings the whole time.

I ended up calling my mom the next morning and telling her that Mutsuki was in the middle of writing an important report, and didn't have time to meet for dinner.

It was one evening about four days later that Mutsuki came back with a swollen jaw. The corner of his mouth was a deep bloody purple, and there was a cut on his lower lip. He said Kon had punched him. Suddenly a terrible thought occurred to me.

"You didn't try to break up with him, did you?"

Mutsuki shook his head. No, that wasn't it.

"Thank god," I said, my hand to my heart. I looked at Mutsuki's cut again. He tried to laugh it off as nothing worth worrying about, but behind his smiling face I could tell he was actually suffering.

"So what was it, then?"

Mutsuki didn't answer. Suddenly he said he'd tell me a story about Kon. It was the first time he'd ever volunteered one.

"About what?"

"About what brought us together."

"Wait, wait! I have to get myself set up!" I went and got a glass, two ice cubes, and a bottle of Irish whiskey. "Okay. I'm ready. Fire away."

"Kon was in high school, and I had just started med school," Mutsuki said. "But we'd always been really close. We were neighbors, remember. More like brothers than anything else, I suppose. You probably don't know this about Kon, but he was in the art society. He was pretty good, won prizes and stuff. Anyway, one day—actually, in the middle of the night—Kon comes climbing up to my window as usual, and asks if it's okay to do some painting in my room. He had a backpack with him, with all his art stuff inside: brushes, oils, bits of cloth, canvas. Everything. And he had this rope with him too, tied to his ankle, and he was using it to drag his easel up behind him as well. It was a full moon that night, and he was like some kid who'd run away from home. After that, he used to come over every night to paint in my room. A week or so went by, and the picture was finished. I was expecting it to be something special, a portrait of me or something. But it turned out to be a painting of the night sky. All these millions of stars scattered across the darkness. That's all. 'This is for you,' he said. I don't know whether you'll understand this, but I *knew*. I knew that his painting was a love

letter, a desperate love letter meant for me. We'd been friends
for so long. I was suffering, too; we'd both reached the point
where we didn't know what to do. The sky in his painting was so
vast, so calm, so quiet. And that was when things got started
between us, that night."

Mutsuki finished his story and took a sip of whiskey.

"So, did he smell like coke?" I asked.

Mutsuki gave a dry smile. "I don't really remember," he said.
"I had other things on my mind."

I went out onto the veranda with my glass of whiskey. I
could see the trains running in the distance, regular streams of
well-lit windows passing through the night, and it didn't seem
possible that there could be real people behind them. A painting
of stars scattered across the sky. Wow. No matter how hard I
tried, I'd never be able to take Kon's place. I wondered what
had made Mutsuki tell me about it now, out of the blue.

Mutsuki came in the next morning while I was still half-
asleep. He had already been up for a while. He was standing
next to my bed, staring at my face. It was kind of a creepy feeling. I half-opened my eyes and said good morning.

"Morning." He was smiling as usual, a postcard in his right
hand. "You want some coffee?" I said yes.

Mutsuki put the postcard on the bed and headed back into
the kitchen. "I'll make you some. The postcard's from Kon. I

found it in the mailbox with the morning paper."

"Oh." I got up and read the postcard. There was no stamp. It was written in black ink in a neat, clear hand.

Dear Mutsuki & Shoko Kishida,

I'm going away for a while. I don't know where yet. Maybe the north of Japan, maybe South America, maybe Okinawa, maybe Africa. Please don't worry about me. Take care.

Kon

I had to read it five times before I understood what had happened.

WHERE WATERS RUN

• •

One month now since Kon left. One irritating, confusing month.

The first week, Shoko was more upset than I was. She was the one who went looking for him on campus and at his parents' place. She called the airport and asked them to look for Kon's name on the passenger list of every departing flight. (She failed to turn up a single clue either at his parents' or at the university, and, not surprisingly, the operators at the airport didn't take her seriously.)

And then she started in on me ("I want to know what you said to Kon," she demanded), blaming me for everything and constantly looking to pick a fight, until she lost hope and gave up.

"It's over," she said. Her nose was red. She didn't say anything more. She looked weak, like someone who had given up something extremely important.

Strangely enough, I was relatively calm that week. I was too busy worrying about Shoko close at hand, and didn't have much time to think about Kon, who was somewhere far away. This made me realize all the more just how secure a place Kon had in my life and how much I trusted him. Part of me was also taking him for granted. I knew there was no way he'd just go off and leave me.

At the end of that first week came a sharp turnabout. I came home from the hospital to find dinner ready and waiting (well, actually it was just some reheated rolls in a basket and a big plate of freshly rinsed pears and grapes).

Shoko smiled cheerfully. "Welcome home," she said. "I've been waiting. I'm so hungry!" She splashed some California wine into a huge glass. "I've decided to give up looking for Kon." She was bubbling over, and unusually chatty. Her skin was starting to turn pink. "Kon must have his reasons, after all."

I asked her what had happened.

"Nothing," she said, tearing off some wheat bread. "I just thought it'd be a good idea to deal with some troublesome little details while he's away on his trip."

"Troublesome little details?" I asked, but as usual Shoko didn't bother to reply.

"Kon was probably thinking the same thing, and that's why he went away."

"Have you seen him?" My voice came out sounding harsh, and Shoko looked a little shocked. She shook her head.

"How could I have seen him? You scared me, yelling like that all of a sudden."

"Sorry," I said.

For a moment Shoko looked lonely. "You don't have to be sorry," she said, and turned away. "He'll be fine. He's a pretty tough customer."

"Yeah," I said quietly. That was true. He was tough.

We ate the bread and fruit, and finished the bottle of wine in less than an hour.

Shoko's conviction that everything was going to turn out for the best grew stronger by the day. In contrast, I was feeling more and more anxious all the time. One by one she set about tidying up all those "troublesome little details" in an extremely businesslike manner. First she made up with Mizuho, announcing that Kon was now out of the picture. Before long, of course, the news reached Shoko's parents and they asked us over to the house. I sat on the floor in formal style before my father-in-law and gave him a full report. What the hell was I doing? It felt weird, kneeling there with my hands on my knees. Why did I have to report to him about our private affairs? It all seemed so fake: the solemn look on my father-in-law's face and my mother-in-law's constant motion, nervously standing up, sitting down, and shuffling in and out of the room with fresh supplies of tea and snacks.

"So you managed to come to terms with things then, did

you, managed to sort out your feelings?" my father-in-law asked. I shrank back like a little child.

I answered yes. "I'm sorry we've caused you so much trouble." What was this, anyway? What the hell was I doing in that house?

"And it's not just because Kon went away, you know," Shoko said, seated beside me. "It was probably the other way around. Our decision made him leave."

My mother-in-law nodded repeatedly, and answered on behalf of my father-in-law. "Oh yes, we understand that, of course. I knew right away that last time you came over, Shoko. I don't think your father ever really doubted it either. But with something like this it's only prudent to make absolutely sure...."

After that, they treated us to an eel dinner, and we drank some sake they'd ordered all the way from Kanazawa. Needless to say, my father-in-law wasn't exactly in the best mood ever, but at the end of the evening he did shake my hand and ask me to "take care of her." It was a sign of his confidence in me, but at the same time I knew it was a warning too.

We got into the car. I opened the sun roof (Shoko always got carsick, so by now it was second nature to me), and put a cassette in the deck. It was one of Shoko's favorites, the soundtrack to *Die Leser*, a collection of eight Beethoven pieces. Her parents stood side by side as they saw us off. I waved goodbye and then put my foot on the accelerator. We drove away slowly up and down the windy hillside slopes of the residential area where Shoko's parents lived.

"Was that okay?"

Shoko nodded in response to my voice, her eyes focused straight ahead of us. "Thank you," she said quietly. Her earlier cheerfulness was gone now, and I knew she was starting to feel depressed. We hit the main road, and Shoko's frown deepened as the dial on the speedometer climbed higher and higher.

"Don't worry. I'll keep my promise."

"Okay," I said. It was more of a compromise than a promise. The deal was that if I saw her parents and gave them the "evidence," Shoko would forget about artificial insemination for a while. It was Shoko's idea. She called it a "business arrangement," but it still made me sad. Business arrangement or friendly promise, this was no way to proceed.

The day before Kon disappeared, I had a call on the internal line summoning me to the Gynecology Office. Kakii's voice was trembling with rage. Wondering what it was all about, I hurried over to the office and arrived to find Kon sitting in Kakii's chair. Kakii himself was standing next to him. Fortunately, there were no other doctors around.

"Mutsuki! I want him out of here this instant." Kakii's face was pale with fury.

"What have you done?" I said.

Kon looked away coolly. "Nothing. It was only a joke. No big deal."

But Kakii was livid. "This is a hospital for God's sake! I've had enough of your infantilism."

Infantile?

"What did you do?" I asked again. Judging from the way Kakii was carrying on, I was sure it must have been something pretty terrible.

"This." Kon gestured with his chin toward the desk, where a rubber toy about seven centimeters across was sitting. It was a lurid yellow-and-green frog.

"You're kidding."

I looked back and forth between Kakii and Kon. They were both sulking now. It was ridiculous. The tension ebbed from me.

"I don't believe this."

Everyone is afraid of something. For Kakii, it was frogs. A long time ago, he had admitted to me that he was more scared of them than he was of women. But still, there was no need for him to flip out like that. Kon had obviously been up to his old tricks again. Coming all the way to the hospital just to play some dumb joke.

"Nice one," I said.

They were both being infantile. I found myself laughing instead of getting mad, and Kon had a smug look on his face now that it looked as though I was taking his side.

"You're both crazy," Kakii said, lowering his head. I thought he was going to start crying. His face had looked so pale when I first came in. Now it was the more familiar bright red.

"Now you really look like a ripe persimmon," Kon said. He was playing on Kakii's name, *kaki* being the word for persimmon.

I was about to say something, but Kakii beat me to it. He was glaring at Kon now with open contempt. "I'm not surprised Shoko's going crazy," he said with disgust. "I sympathize with her."

Apparently I wasn't alone in feeling upset that Kakii had brought Shoko into this. "What's that supposed to mean?" Kon said.

"Shoko came in to see me on Monday," Kakii replied. He sounded triumphant.

"I know. She told me herself."

"Did she tell you what we talked about?"

"Of course." I glanced over at Kon. Even if I asked him to leave now, he certainly wasn't the type to oblige. "Artificial insemination, right? It's better to do it while you're still young, then the success rates are higher with frozen sperm. All that stuff."

"That's what *I* told *her*," said Kakii. "What Shoko came to discuss wasn't quite as general as that. It was more concrete.

Kind of bizarre, in fact." Kakii looked serious. He was quiet for a moment.

"It's rather difficult to say," he started.

"Say it."

He was silent.

Kakii could be difficult at times like this. It took about five minutes of coaxing and cajoling before he finally spilled the beans.

"What Shoko wanted to discuss…well, it's kind of embarrassing, but she wanted to know if it was possible to mix your sperm with Kon's in a test tube. For fertilization. Her idea was that that way the baby would belong to all three of you."

I was stunned. Was such a thing even possible? No one said a thing for a minute or more.

It was then that Kon punched me suddenly in the jaw. He wasn't holding anything back. I fell against the desk from the strength of the blow, and sent a stack of papers crashing to the floor.

"You should never have married Shoko-chan in the first place if you were going to make her so unhappy!" His outburst seemed sincere—so unlike the usual Kon. And at last I understood what should have been obvious. It wasn't only Shoko who had been suffering all this time. Kon had been in pain too.

It was the day after that incident that Kon disappeared.

I parked the car in the lot, unfastened my seat belt, popped the tape out of the deck, closed the sun roof, and turned off the engine. Shoko still made no move to get out of the car.

"Shoko?"

She had hardly said a word on the way home, either. The music floated quietly into the confined space of the car, and Shoko just sat there without saying a word. She was frowning.

"Do you miss him?" she asked, without looking at me. "Do you miss Kon now that he's gone?" I glanced across at her. She looked really tense. She was staring through the windshield out into the darkness beyond.

"Yes, I miss him," I answered honestly. "But I feel more lost than lonely," I added. There was no doubt that what I was feeling was more than just loneliness. It was indeed an emotion I couldn't find words to describe, and it was affecting my whole life. It went much deeper than mere loneliness. I still couldn't come to accept Kon's absence. Perhaps this was what a twin went through when the other twin died.

I suddenly realized that Shoko was sobbing. Her face was contorted with pain and suffering, and she was wailing like a child.

I told her I was sorry, but Shoko covered her face with her hands and started sobbing even harder. "Don't apologize," she managed to squeeze out between gulps of air. "It's no one's fault. There's nothing we can do."

She cried so painfully. I gave her a hug, and she threw her arms around my neck—with surprising strength, crying still. Her breath and her tears burned my face and neck. She clutched at my hair with her hands, and stayed in that position for a long time, crying. It felt as though someone was biting into my neck. I wasn't thinking about anything anymore. I simply held Shoko's soft, defenseless body in my arms. It felt like an eternity, a time unto itself.

"I feel a little better now."

I let go. She looked a little embarrassed, but her eyes were smiling.

"There's nothing we can do though, right? I miss him too."

She seemed revitalized as she wiped her wet face with the back of her hand. And then, with inexplicable confidence, she announced that Kon was about to came back anyway.

We got out of the car. The September night air was soft and cool, and the gentle breeze dried Shoko's tears from my neck.

Back in the apartment, I took a shower and then went out on the veranda to look at the stars. Shoko was pouring tea into the potted plant. She was singing in an almost unnaturally loud voice. "Baby's Little Ears." Usually she would have joined me out there, a glass of whiskey in hand, but tonight she didn't come near me, and I couldn't find the right moment to step back into the room myself. How funny that we were both embarrassed about that embrace in the car. I stared at my reflection in the window, and touched my right cheek with my finger. I tried to remember the feel of Shoko's slender white hands, her heated and tearful voice, her lips. Cepheus and Cassiopeia shone brightly in the sky.

"Let's all go out on trips together when Kon gets back. Picnics and stuff. Okay?" Suddenly, there she was at my side.

It happened three days later, on the last Sunday of September. I opened my eyes to find the bed next to mine empty. I went into the living room and saw a teddy bear holding a small card. Happy Anniversary, it said. Anniversary? I went back into the bedroom and looked at the calendar. September 30th. It was the day we first met.

I had meant to remember such things, and I was irritated with myself for forgetting, and with Kon, who had distracted me. I walked around the apartment, expecting to find Shoko, but she wasn't in the bathroom, or on the veranda, or in the kitchen, and to top it all off, the *yucca elephantipes* and the Cézanne were both missing. Without them, the living room didn't feel like ours anymore.

The phone rang. I picked it up.

"Morning!" Shoko's voice came burbling down the line. "It's such a nice day. I'm downstairs. We thought we'd throw a party. Room 202. Hurry up and come down here, I have a present for you."

"Hey, pushy, whose place is it? Room 202?"

But naturally Shoko didn't respond to that. She kept talking. "You have to get dressed up, okay? And can you bring the champagne stirrer? And some canned stuff. You know—sardines, asparagus, pâté."

I put all the things she asked for in a paper bag and went to get myself ready. Thirty minutes later, I went downstairs. I didn't know what kind of party it was, but I thought a tie would be overdoing it even if Shoko had asked me to dress up. I put on a tweed jacket over a T-shirt.

The door opened as soon as I pressed the bell, and Kon appeared from inside. He had a huge red ribbon tied around his head. He was wearing jeans and a navy blue blazer of some kind. For Kon this was a major step up towards being properly dressed.

"KON!" I exclaimed. I must have sounded insane.

"This is your present," Shoko said, smiling as she came over next to him. Then I realized what the red ribbon was all about.

"Happy Anniversary," Kon laughed. He turned to Shoko and said in a barely audible voice, "As if I would ever really leave him!"

The radio was tuned to a soft rock station, and the *yucca elephantipes* and the Cézanne were by the table.

"Let's have a toast," Shoko said.

"Explain yourselves!" I said. "If this is supposed to be some big joke, some kind of plot or something...." I tried to sound angry, but ended up just sounding astounded and foolish.

"The trip only lasted a week," Shoko said, looking at Kon as if they were sharing a secret.

"I don't have enough money for anything longer than that, anyway," Kon added. "As if I could ever make it to Africa or even China. I thought things would be cleared up in a week, but when I called Shoko-chan, she said she hadn't been able to do anything at all. I was kinda surprised."

"We were worried to death about you," Shoko said, looking to me for confirmation. Yes, to say the least, I thought.

"And so you both kept quiet about it until now?"

"Yep."

Shoko and Kon nodded cheerfully, as if they saw nothing wrong in what they had done. "We don't think there's anything wrong with a few little lies."

I didn't know what to say. Great. Just great.

"Shoko-chan made all the arrangements and I moved in here the day before yesterday. I had to take out a loan to cover the rent. I guess I'll have to take on another part-time job." Grinning, he added: "And I guess this makes us neighbors."

Was this a joke? What was going to happen next?

There was a huge mound of vegetables in a bowl on the table.

"Up until now he's been staying in this capsule hotel near

Ogikubo station. I went to visit him there, and man it was so strange. Freaked me out." Shoko started going through the bag I had brought. "Have you ever stayed in one of those places?" she asked.

Kon opened the champagne and I stirred up three glasses.

"Here's to Kon for coming back safe and sound, and to the three of us, for our first year together," Shoko said.

"And here's to the happy couple, for becoming independent at last!" added Kon. I lifted my glass and looked around the room again. White walls, white ceiling, a huge electric fan. Just like our place. A familiar old pop song started playing on the radio as we all stood there drinking our champagne. Billy Joel.

I felt like crying. Love alone helped us get through life. Without it, life was simply too haphazard.

What was this song, anyway? It was the first song off his first album. The melody alone was enough to make you want to cry.

"*She's Got a Way*, right?" It was as if Kon had read my mind.

And this is what our life was going to be like tomorrow, the day after tomorrow, and the day after that. I poured myself another glass of champagne.

"You can make up for it and give me two presents next year," Shoko said. Before her, the Cézanne painting was smiling more happily than ever.

AFTERWORD

I try to be careful, but I sometimes fall in love.

This book is intended to be a simple love story. About falling in love, about understanding that other person. My belief is that every human being is alone and lonely.

The title, *Twinkle Twinkle*, I took from a poem by Yasuo Irizawa.

Two of the chapter titles were taken from paintings, *The Sleepers and One That Watcheth* and *The Star-sower*. I forget who painted the latter, but the former is by Simeon Solomon. It depicts a group of three people, men and women, cheek to cheek—a strange and beautiful painting. Simeon Solomon, who lived in the 19th century, was cast out by the art world when he was suspected of homosexuality.

To be perfectly honest with you, I think it's reckless to love and trust another person. It's clearly foolhardy.

I'd like it very much if the many daredevils who go ahead anyway enjoyed this book.